STELLA DUFFY has written thirteen novels, over fifty short stories and ten plays. In addition to her writing work she is a theatre-maker and founder of the Fun Palaces national and international campaign for arts, sciences and culture, for everyone, everywhere.

EVERYTHING IS MOVING, EVERYTHING IS JOINED

The Selected Stories of Stella Duffy

Stella Duffy

SALT

CROMER

PUBLISHED BY SALT

12 Norwich Road, Cromer, Norfolk NR27 0AX United Kingdom

Printed in Great Britain by Clays Ltd, St Ives plc

Typeset in Sabon 10/13

ISBN 978 1 907773 05 1 paperback

1 3 5 7 9 8 6 4 2

For my friend, colleague and Fun Palaces partner,
Sarah-Jane Rawlings,
thank you for diving in.

CONTENTS

EVERYTHING IS MOVING, EVERYTHING IS JOINED

MARTHA GRACE

Martha Grace is what in the old days would have been termed a 'fine figure of a woman'. Martha Grace is big-boned and strong. Martha Grace could cross a city, climb a mountain range, swim an ocean – and still not break into a sweat. She has wide thighs and heavy breasts and child-bearing hips, though in her fifty-eight years there has been no call for labour-easing width. Martha Grace has a low-slung belly, gently downed, soft as clean brushed cotton. Martha Grace lives alone and grows herbs and flowers and strange foreign vegetables in her marked-out garden. She plants by the light of the full moon. When she walks down the street people move out of her way, children giggle behind nervous hands, adults cast sidelong glances and wonder. When she leaves a room people whisper 'dyke' and 'witch', though Martha Grace is neither. Martha Grace loves alone, pleasuring her own sweetly rolling flesh, clean oiled skin soft beneath her wide mouth. Martha Grace could do with getting out more.

Tim Culver is sixteen. He is big for his age and loved. Football star, athlete, and clever too. Tim Culver could have his pick of any girl in the class. And several of their mothers. One or two of their older brothers. If he was that way inclined. Which he isn't. Certainly not. Tim Culver isn't that kind of boy. Tim Culver is just too clean. And good. And right. And ripe. Good enough for girls, too clean for boys. Tim Culver, for a bet, turns up at Martha Grace's house on a quiet Saturday afternoon, friends giggling round the corner, wide smirk on his handsome not-yet-grown face. He offers himself as an odd-job man. And then comes back to her house almost every weekend for the next three years. He says it is to help her out. She's a single woman, she's not that bad, a bit strange maybe, but no worse than his Grandma in the years before she died. And she's not that old really. Or that fat. Just big. Different to the women he's used to. She talks to him differently. And anyway, Martha Grace pays well. In two hours at her house he can earn twice what he'd make mowing the lawn for his father, painting houses with his big brother. She doesn't know he's using her, thinks she's paying him the going rate. God knows she never talks to anyone to compare it. It's fine, he knows what he's doing, Tim Culver is in charge, takes no jokes at his own expense. And after a few false starts, failed attempts at schoolboy mockery, the laughing stops, the other kids wish they'd thought to try the mad old bitch for some cash. Tim Culver earns more than any of them, in half the time. But then, he always has been the golden boy.

For Tim, this was meant to be just a one-off. Visit the crazy fat lady, prove his courage to his friends, and then leave, laughing in her face. He does leave laughing. And comes back hungry the next day, wanting more. It takes no time at all to become routine. The knock at the door, the boy standing there, insolent smile and ready cock, hands held out to offer, 'Got any jobs that need doing?'

And Martha did find him work. That first day. No matter how greedy his grin, how firm his young flesh, what else she could see waiting on her doorstep that young Tim Culver couldn't even guess at. Mow the lawn. Clean out the pond. Mend the broken fence. Then maybe she thought he should come inside, clean up, rest a while, as she fixed him a drink, found her purse, offered a fresh clean note. And herself.

At first, Tim Culver wasn't sure he understood her correctly.

'So Tim, have you had sex yet?'

Why would the fat woman be asking him that? What did she know about sex? And did she mean ever as in today, or ever as in ever? Tim Culver blustered, he didn't know how to answer her, of course he'd had sex. The first in his class, and – so the girls said – the best. Tim Culver was not just a shag-merchant like the rest of them. He might fuck a different girl from one Saturday to the next, but he prides himself on knowing a bit about what he's doing. Every girl remembered Tim Culver. Martha Grace remembered Tim Culver. She'd been watching him. That was the thing about being the mad lady, fat lady, crazy old woman. They watched her all the time, laughed at her. They didn't notice that she was also watching them.

Tim Culver says yes, he has had sex. Of course he's had sex. What does she think he is? Does she think he's a poof? Mad old dyke, what the fuck does she think he is?

Martha Grace explains that she doesn't yet know what he is. That's why he's here. That's why she asked him into her house. So she could find out. Tim Culver knows a challenge when it's thrown his way.

When Tim Culver and Martha Grace fuck, it is like no other time with any other woman. Tim Culver has fucked other women, other girls, plenty of them. He is a local hero after all. Not for him all talk and no action. When Tim Culver says he has been there, done that, you know he really means it. But with Martha Grace it is different. For a start there is not fucker and fuckee. And she does talk to him, encourages him, welcomes him, incites him. Martha Grace makes Tim Culver more of the man he would have himself be. Laid out against her undulating flesh, Tim Culver's young toned body is hero-strong, he is capable of any feat of daring, the gentlest acts of kindness. Tim Culver and Martha Grace are making love. Tim Culver drops deep into her soft skin and wide body and is more than happy to lose himself there, give himself away.

Before he leaves, she feeds him. Fresh bread she baked that morning, kneading the dough beneath her fat hands as she kneaded his flesh just minutes ago. She spreads thick yellow butter on the soft bread and layers creamy honey on top, sweet from her hands to his mouth. Then back to her mouth as they kiss and she wipes the crumbs from his shirt front. She is tidier than he is, does not like to see him make a mess. Would not normally bear the thought of breadcrumbs on her pristine floor. But that Tim Culver is delicious, and the moisture in her mouth at the sight of him drives away thoughts of sweeping and scrubbing and cleaning. At least until he is gone, at least until she is alone again. For now, Martha Grace is all abandon. Fresh and warm in a sluttish kitchen. After another half hour in the heat by the stove, Tim Culver has to go. His friends will wonder what has happened to him. His mother will be expecting him in for dinner. He has to shower, get dressed again, go out. He has young people to meet and a pretty redhead to pick up at eight thirty. Tim Culver leaves with a crisp twenty in his pocket and fingers the note, volunteering to come back next

Saturday. Martha Grace thinks, stares at the boy, half smiles with a slow incline of her head, she imagines there will be some task for him to do. Two pm. Sharp. Don't be late. Tim Culver nods, he doesn't usually take orders. But then, this feels more like an offer. One his aching body won't let him refuse.

She watches him walk away, turns back to look at the mess of her kitchen. Martha Grace spends the next three hours cleaning up. Scrubbing down the floor, the table. Changing the sheets, wiping surfaces, picking up after herself. When she sits down to her own supper she thinks about the boy out for the night, spending her money on the little redhead. She sighs, he could buy the girl a perfectly adequate meal with that money. If such a girl would ever eat a whole meal anyway. Poor little painfully thin babies that they are. Living shiny magazine half lives of self-denial and want. Martha Grace chooses neither. Before she goes to sleep, Martha notes down the visit and the payment in her accounts book. She has not paid the boy for sex. That would have been wrong. She paid him for the work he'd done. The lawn, the fence, the pond. The sex was simply an extra.

Extra-regular. On Saturday afternoons, after winter football practice, after summer runs, late from long holiday mornings sleeping off the after-effects of teenage Friday night, Tim Culver walks to the crazy lady's house. Pushes open the gate he oiled last weekend, walks past the rosemary and comfrey and yarrow he pruned in early spring, takes out the fresh-cut key she has given him, lets himself into the dark hallway he will paint next holiday, and walks upstairs. Martha Grace is waiting for him. She has work for Tim Culver to do.

Martha Grace waits in her high, soft bed. She is naked.

Her long grey hair falls around her shoulders, usually it is pulled back tight so that even Martha's cheekbones protrude from the flesh of her round cheeks, now the hair covers the upper half of her voluminous breasts, deep red and wide, the nipples raised beneath the scratch of her grey hair. Tim Culver nods at Martha Grace, almost smiles, walks past the end of her bed to the bathroom. The door is left open so Martha Grace can watch him from her bed. He takes off his sweaty clothes, peels them from skin still hot and damp, then lowers himself into the bath she has ready for him. Dried rose petals float on the surface of the water, rosemary, camomile and other herbs he doesn't recognise. Tim Culver sinks beneath the water and rises up again, all clean and ready for bed.

In bed. Tim Culver sinks into her body. Sighs in relief and pleasure. He has been a regular visitor to her home and her flesh for almost three years now. The place where he lays with Martha Grace's soft, fat body is as much home to him as his mother's table or the room he shares with an old friend now that he has moved away. Tim Culver has graduated from high school fucks to almost-romance with college girls. Pretty, thin, clever, bright and shiny college girls. Lots of them. Tim Culver is a good looking boy and clearly well worth the bodies these girls are offering. This is the time of post-feminism. They want to fuck him because he is good looking and charming and will make a great story tomorrow in the lunch-time canteen. And Tim is perfectly happy for this to be the case. The girls may revel in the glories of their fiercely free sexuality, Tim just wants to get laid every night. Everyone's happy. And the girls are definitely happy. It's not just that Tim Culver is good looking and clever and fit. He also, really really, knows what he's doing.

Which is more than can be said for most of the football team. Tim Culver is a young man of depth and experience. And of course it is good for Tim too, to be seen to be fucking at this rate. To be this much the all-round popular guy. But as he lies awake next to another fine, thin, lithe, little body he recognises a yearning in his skin. He is tired of fucking girls who ache in every bone of their arched-back body to be told they are the best. Tired of screwing young women who constantly demand that he praise their emaciated ribs, their skeletal cheekbones, their tight and wiry arms. Weary of the nearly-relationships with would-be poet girls who want to torment him with their deep insights into pain and suffering and sex and music. Tim Culver is exhausted by the college girls he fucks.

They are not soft these young women at college, and they need so much attention. Even when they don't say so out loud, they need so much attention. Tim learnt this in his first week away from home. Half asleep and his back turned to the blonde of the evening, her soft sobs drew him from the rest he so needed. No there was nothing wrong, yes it had been fine, he'd been great, she'd come, of course it was all ok. She wasn't crying, not really, it was just . . . and this in a small voice, not the voice she'd come with, or the voice she'd picked him up with, or the voice she'd use to re-tell the best parts of the story tomorrow, but . . . was she all right? Did he like her? Was she pretty enough? Thin enough? Good enough? Only this one had dared to speak aloud, but he felt it seeping out of all the others. Every single one of them, eighteen, nineteen year old girls, each one oozing please-praise-me from their emaciated, emancipated pores. But not Martha Grace.

With Martha Grace Tim can rest. Maybe Martha Grace

needs him, Tim cannot tell for certain. She likes him, he knows that. Certainly she wants him, hungers for him. As he now knows he hungers for her. But if she needs him, it is only Tim that she needs. His body, his presence, his cock. She does not need his approval, his blessing, his constant, unending hymn of there-there. And maybe that is because he has none to give. She is fat. And old. And weird. What could he approve of? What is there to approve of? Nothing at all. They both know that. And so it is, that when Tim comes home to Martha, there is rest along with exertion. There is ease in the fucking. Martha Grace knows who she is, what she is. She demands nothing extra of him, what sanctions of beauty or thinness, or perfection could he give her anyway? She has none of those and so, as Tim acknowledges to himself in surprise and pleasure, she is easier to be with than the bone-stabbing stick figure girls at school. And softer. And wider. And more comfortable. It is better in that house, that bed, against that heavy body. Martha Grace is not eighteen, and a part of Tim Culver sits up shocked and amused – he realises he loves her for it. The rest of Tim Culver falls asleep, his heavy head on her fat breast. Martha Grace smells the other women in his hair.

One day Tim Culver brings Martha Grace a new treat. He knows of her appetite for food and drink and him, he understands her cravings and her ever-hungry mouth. He loves her ever-hungry mouth. He brings gifts from the big city, delicatessen offerings, imported chocolates and preserves. Wines and liquors. He has the money. He is not a poor student. Martha Grace sees to that. This time the home-from-college boy brings her a new gift. Martha Grace had tried marijuana years ago, it didn't suit her, she liked to feel in control, didn't understand the desire to take a drug that made one lose control, the opposite of her wanting. She has told Tim this, explained about her past experiences, how she came to be the woman she is today. Has shared with Tim each and every little step that took her from the wide open world to wide woman in a closed house. And he has nodded and understood. Or appeared to do so. At the very least he has listened, and that is new and precious to Martha. So she is willing to trust him. Scared but willing. And this time, Tim brings home cocaine. Martha is shocked and secretly delighted. But she is the older woman, he still just a student, she must maintain some degree of adult composure. She tells him to put it away, take it back to school, throw it out. Tells him off, delivers a sharp rebuke, a reprimand and then sends him to bed. Her bed. Tim walks upstairs smiling. He leaves the thin wrap on the hall table. Martha Grace watches him walk away, feels the smirk from the back of his head, threatens a slap which she knows he wants anyway. Her hand reaches out for the wrap. Such a small thing and so much fuss. She pictures the naked boy upstairs. Man. Young man. In her bed. Hears again the fuss she knows it would cause. Hears again as he calls her, taunting from the room above. She is hungry and wanting. Her soft hand closes around the narrow strip of folded paper and she follows his trail of clothes upstairs, clucking like a disparaging mother hen at the lack of tidiness, folding, putting away. Getting into bed, putting to rights.

Tim Culver lays out a long thin line on Martha Grace's heavy stomach. It wobbles as she breathes in, breathes out, the small ridge of cocaine mountain sited on her skin, creamy white avalanche grains tumbling with her sigh. He inhales cocaine and the clean, fleshy smell of Martha. And both are inspirations for him. Now her turn. She rolls the boy over on to his stomach, lays out an uncertain line from his low waist to the soft hairs at the curve of his arse. She is slow and deliberate, new to this, does not want to get it wrong. Tim is finding it hard to stay face down, wants to burrow himself into the flesh of Martha Grace, not the unyielding mattress. She lays her considerable weight out along his legs, hers dangling off the end of the bed, breasts to buttocks and inhales coke and boy and, not for the first time in her life, the thick iron smell of bloody desire. Then she reaches up to stretch herself out against him full length, all of her pressing down into all of him. The weight of her flesh against his back and legs has Tim Culver reaching for breath. He wonders if this is what it is like for the little girls he fucks at college. He a tall, strong young man and they small, brittle beneath him. At some point in the sex he always likes to lie on top. To feel himself above the young women, all of him stretched out against the twisted paper and bones of the young girl skin, narrow baby-woman hips jutting sharp into his abdomen, reminding him of what he has back at home, Martha waiting for the weekend return. He likes it when, breath forced from the thin lungs beneath him, they whisper the fuck in half-caught breaths. Tim has always been told it feels good, the heaviness, the warmth, the strong body laid out and crushing down, lip to lip, cock to cunt, tip to toe. He hopes it is like this for the narrow young women he lays on top of. Tim Culver likes this. He is surprised by the feeling, wonders if it is just the coke or the addition of physical pressure, Martha's wide weight gravity-heavy against his back, pushing his body down, spreading him out. Is wondering still when she slides her hand in between his legs and up to his cock. Is wondering no longer when he comes five minutes later, Martha still on his back, mouth to his neck, teeth to his tanned skin. Her strength, her weight, like no other female body he has felt. He thinks then for a brief moment about the gay boys he knows (barely, acquaintances), wonders if this is what it is like for them too. But wonders only briefly; momentary sex-sense identification with the thin young women is a far enough stretch for a nineteen-year-old small town boy.

They did not take cocaine together again. Martha liked it, but Martha would rather be truly in control than amphetamine-convinced by the semblance of control. Besides that, she had, as usual, prepared a post-sex snack for that afternoon. Glass of sweet dessert wine and rich cherry cake, the cherries individually pitted by her own fair, fat hands the evening before, left to soak in sloe gin all night, waiting for Tim's mouth to taste them, just as she was. But after the drugs and the sex and then some more of the bitter powder, neither had an appetite for food. They had each other and cocaine and then Tim left. Martha didn't eat until the evening, and alone, and cold. Coke headache dulling the tip of her left temple. She could cope with abandon. She could certainly enjoy a longer fuck, a seemingly more insatiable desire from the young man of her fantasies come true. She could, on certain and specified occasions, even put up with a ceding of power. But she would not again willingly submit to self-inflicted loss of appetite. That was just foolish.

It went on. Three months more, then six, another three. Seasons back to where they started. Tim Culver and Martha

Grace. The mask of garden chores and DIY tasks, then the fucking and the feeding and the financial recompense. Then even, one late afternoon in winter, dark enough outside for both to kid themselves they had finally spent a night together, an admission of love. It comes first from Tim. Surprising himself. He's held it in all this time, found it hard to believe it was true, but knows the miracle fact as it falls from his gratified mouth:

'Martha, I love you.'

Martha Grace smiles and nods.

'Tim, I love you.'

Not 'back'. Or 'too'. Just love.

A month more. Tim Culver and Martha Grace loving. In love. Weekend adoration and perfect.

And then Martha thinks she will maybe pay him a visit. Tim always comes to her. She will go to his college. Surprise him. Take a picnic, all his favourite foods and her. Martha Grace's love in a basket. She packs a pie – tender beef and slow-cooked sweet onion, the chunky beef slightly bloody in the middle, just the way Tim likes it. New bread pitted with dark green olives, Tim's favourite. Fresh shortbread and strawberry tarts with imported out-of-season berries. A thermos of mulled wine, the herbs and spices her own blend from the dark cupboard beneath her stairs. She dresses carefully and wears lipstick, culled from the back of a drawer and an intentionally forgotten time of made-up past. Walks into town, camomile-washed hair flowing about her shoulders, head held high, best coat, pretty shoes – party shoes. Travels on the curious bus, catches a cab to the college.

And all the time Martha Grace knows better. Feels at the

lowest slung centre of her belly the terror of what is to come. Doesn't know how she can do this even as she does it. Wants to turn back with every step, every mile. Knows in her head it can not be, in her stomach it will not work. But her stupid fat heart sends her stumbling forwards anyway. She climbs down from the bus and walks to the coffee shop he has mentioned. Where he sits with his friends, passing long slow afternoons of caffeine and chocolate and drawled confidences. He is not there and Martha Grace sits alone at a corner table for an hour. Another. And then Tim Culver arrives. With a gaggle of laughing others. He is brash and young. Sits backwards across the saddle of his chair. Makes loud noises, jokes, creates a rippling guffaw of youthful enjoyment all around him. He does not notice Martha Grace sat alone in the corner, a pale crumble of dried cappuccino froth at the corner of her mouth. But eventually, one of his friends does. Points her out quietly to another. There are sniggers, sideways glances. Martha Grace could not be more aware of her prominence. But still she sits, knowing better and hoping for more. Then Tim sees her, his attention finally drawn from the wonder of himself to the absurdity of the fat woman in the corner. And Tim looks up, directly at Martha Grace, right into her pale grey eyes and he stands and he walks towards her and his friends are staring after him, whooping and hollering, catcalls and cheers, and then he has stopped by her table and he sits beside Martha Grace and reaches towards her and touches the line of her lips, moves in, licks away the dried milk crust. He stands again, bows a serious little bow, and walks back to his table of friends. Who stand and cheer and push forward the young girls to kiss, pretty girls, thin girls. Tim Culver has kissed Martha Grace in public and it has made him a hero. And made the fool of Martha Grace. She tries to leave the café, tries to walk out unnoticed but her bulk is stuck in the corner arrangement of too-small chairs and shin-splitting low table, her feet clatter against a leaning tray, her heavy arms and shaking hands cannot hold the hamper properly, it falls to her feet and the food rolls out. Pie breaks open, chunks of bloody meat spill across the floor, strawberries that were cool and fresh are now hot and sweating, squashed beneath her painfully pretty shoes as she runs from the room, every action a humiliation, every second another pain. Eventually Martha Grace turns her great bulk at the coffee shop door and walks away down the street, biting the absurd lipstick from her stupid, stupid lips as she goes, desperate to break into a lumbering run, forcing her idiotic self to move slowly and deliberately through the pain. And all the way down the long street, surrounded by strangers and tourists and scrabbling children underfoot, she feels Tim's eyes boring into the searing blush on the back of her neck.

Neither mention the visit. The next weekend comes and goes. Martha is a little cool, somewhat distant. Tim hesitant, uncertain. Wondering whether to feel shame or guilt and then determining on neither when he sees Martha's fear that he might mention what has occurred. Both skirt around their usual routine, there are no jobs to be done, no passion to linger over, the sex is quick and not easy. Tim dresses in a hurry, Martha stays cat-curled in bed, face half-hidden beneath her pillow, she points to the notes on her dresser, Tim takes only half the cash. Pride hurt, vanity exposed, Martha promises herself she will get over it. Pick herself up, get on. Tim need never know how hurt she felt. How stupid she knows herself to have been. The weekend after will be better, she'll prepare a surprise for him, make a real treat, an offering to get things back to where they had been before. Then Martha Grace will be herself again.

Saturday morning and Martha Grace is preparing a special dish for Tim. She knows his taste. He likes berry fruits, loves chocolate like any young boy, though unlike most, Martha Grace has taught him the joy of real chocolate, dark and shocking. She will make him a deep tart of black berries and melted chunks of bitter chocolate, imported from France, ninety percent cocoa solids. She starts early in the day. Purest white flour mixed in the air as she sifts it with organic cocoa. Rich butter, light sugar, cool hands, extra egg to bind the mix. She leaves it in the fridge to chill, the ratio of flour to cocoa so perfect that her pastry is almost black. Then the fruit – blackberries, boysenberries, loganberries, blackcurrants – just simmered with fruit sugar and pure water over the lowest of heat for almost two hours until they are thick syrup and pulp. She skims the scum from the surface, at the very end throws in another handful. This fruit she does not name. These are the other berries she was taught to pick by her mother, in the fresh morning before sunlight has bruised the delicate skin. She leaves the thick fruit mix to cool. Melts the chocolate. Glistening rich black in the shallow pan. When it is viscous and runs slow from the back of her walnut spoon, she drops in warmed essences – almond, vanilla, and a third distilled flavour, stored still, a leftover from her grandmother's days, just in case, for a time of who-knows-and-maybe, hidden at the back of the dark cupboard beneath her stairs. She leaves the pan over hot water, bubbling softly in the cool of her morning kitchen. Lays the pastry out on the marble slab. Rolls it to paper fine. Folds it in on itself and starts again. Seven times more. Then she fits it to the baking dish, fluted edges, heavy base. She bakes the pastry blind and removes from the oven a crisp, dark shell. Pours in warm thick-liquid chocolate, sprinkles over a handful of flaked and toasted almonds, watches them sink into the quicksand black. Her mouth is watering with the heady rich aroma. She knows better than to lick her fingers. Tim Culver likes to lick her fingers. When the chocolate is almost cool, she beats three egg yolks and more sugar into the fruit mixture, pours it slowly over the chocolate, lifts the tart dish and ever so gently places it in the heated oven. She sits for ten minutes, twenty, thirty. She does not wash the dishes while she waits, or wipe flour from her hands, chocolate from her apron. She sits and waits and watches the clock. She cries, one slow fat tear every fifteen seconds. When there are one hundred and sixty tears the tart is done. She takes it from the oven and leaves it to cool. She goes to bed, folds into her own flesh and rocks herself to sleep.

When she wakes Martha checks the tart. It is cool and dark, lifts easily from the case, she sets it on a wide white plate and places it in the refrigerator beside a jug of thick cream. Then she begins to clean. The kitchen, the utensils, the shelves, the oven, the workbench, the floor. Takes herself to the bathroom, strips and places the clothes in a rubbish bag. Scrubs her body under a cold running shower, sand soap and nail brush. Every inch, every fold of flesh and skin. Martha Grace is red-raw clean. The clothes are burnt early that afternoon along with a pile of liquid maple leaves at the bottom of her garden, black skirt, red shirt and the garden matter in seasonal orange rush. Later she rakes over the hot embers, places her hand close to the centre, draws it back just too late, a blister already forming in the centre of her palm. It will do for a reminder. Martha Grace always draws back just too late.

Tim Culver knocks on her door at precisely three forty-five. She has spent a further hour preparing her body for his arrival, oiling and brushing and stroking. She is dressed in a soft black silk that flows over her curves and bulges, hiding some, accentuating others. She has let down her coarse grey hair, reddened her full lips, and has the faintest line of shadow around her pale grey eyes. Tim Culver smiles. Martha Grace is beautiful. He walks into the hall, hands her the thirty red roses he carried behind his back all the way down the street in case she was looking. She was looking. She laughs in delight at the gift, he kisses her and apologies and explanations spill from his mouth. They stumble up the stairs, carrying each other quickly to bed, words unimportant, truth and embarrassment and shame and guilt all gone, just the skin and the fucking and the wide fat flesh. They are so in love and Tim cries out, whimpering with delight at the touch of her yielding skin on his mouth, his chest, his cock. And Martha Grace shuts out all thoughts of past and present, crying only for the now.

When they are done, she takes Tim downstairs. Martha Grace in a light red robe, Tim Culver wrapped in a blanket against the seasonal chill. The curtains are drawn, blinds pulled, lights lowered. She sits the boy at her kitchen table and pours him a glass of wine. And another. She ask him about drugs and Tim is shocked and delighted, yes he does happen to have a wrap in the back pocket of his jeans. Don't worry, stay there, drink another glass. Martha will fetch the wrap. She brings it back to him, lays out the lines, takes in just one half to his every two. He does not question this, is simply pleased she wants to join him in this excess. There is more wine and wanting, cocaine and kissing, fucking on the kitchen table, falling to the just-scrubbed floor. Even with cocaine, the wine and the sex have made him hungry. Martha has a treat. A special tart she baked herself this morning. Pastry and everything. She reaches into the cool refrigerator and brings out her offering. His eyes grow wider at the sight of the plate, pupils dilate still further with spreading saliva in his hungry mouth. She cuts Tim a generous slice, spoons thick cream over it and reaches for a fork. The boy holds out his hand but she pushes it away. She wants to feed him. He wants to be fed.

Tim Culver takes it in. The richness, the darkness, the bitter chocolate and the tart fruit and the sweet syrup and the crisp pastry shell and the cool cream. Tim Culver takes it in and opens his mouth for more. Eyes closed to better savour the texture, the flavours, the glory of this woman spending all morning cooking for him, after what has happened, after how he has behaved. She must love him so much. She must love him as much as he loves her. He opens his eyes to kiss Martha Grace and sees her smiling across at him, another forkful offered, tears spilling down her fat cheeks. He pushes aside the fork and kisses the cheeks, sucks up her tears, promises adoration and apology and forever. Tim Culver is right about forever.

She feeds him half the black tart. He drinks another glass. Leaves a slurred message on a friend's telephone to say he is out with a girl, a babe, a doll. He is having too good a time. He probably won't make it tonight. He expects to stay over tonight. He says this looking at Martha, waiting to see her happiness at the thought that he will stay in her bed, will sleep beside her tonight. Martha Grace smiles an appropriate gratitude and Tim turns his phone off. Martha Grace did not want him to use hers. She said it would not do for his friend to call back on her number. Tim is touched she is thinking of his reputation even now.

She pours more wine. Tim does not see that he is drinking the whole bottle, Martha not at all. He inhales more coke. They fuck again. This time it is less simple. He cannot come. He cuts himself another slice of the tart, eats half, puts it down, gulps a mouthful of wine, licks his finger to wipe sticky crumbs of white powder from the wooden table. Tim Culver is confused. He is tired but wide awake. He is hungry but full. He is slowing-down drunk but wired too. He is in love with Martha Grace but despises both of them for it. He is alive, but only just.

Tim Culver dies of a heart attack. His young healthy heart cannot stand the strain of wine and drugs and fucking – and the special treat Martha had prepared. She pulls his jeans and shirt back on him, moves his body while it is still warm and pliable, lays him on a sheet of spread-out rubbish bags by her back door. She carries him out down the path by her back garden. He is big, but she is bigger, and necessity has made her strong. It is dark. There is no-one to see her stumble through the gate, down the alleyway. No-one to see her leave the half-dressed body in the dark street. No-one to see her gloved hands place the emptied wine bottles by his feet. By the time

Martha Grace kisses his lips they are already cold. He smells of chocolate and wine and sex.

She goes home and for the second time that day, scrubs her kitchen clean. Then she sleeps alone, she will wash in the morning. For now the scent of Tim Culver in her sheets, her hair, her heavy flesh will be enough to keep her warm through the night.

Tim Culver was found the next morning. Cocaine and so much alcohol in his blood. His heart run to a standstill by the excess of youth. There was no point looking for anyone else to blame. No-one saw him stumble into the street. No-one noticed Martha Grace lumber away. His friends confirmed he'd been with a girl that night. The state of his semen-stained clothes confirmed he'd been with a girl that night. At least the police said girl to his parents, whispered whore among themselves. Just another small town boy turned bad by the lights and the nights of the bright city. Maybe further education isn't all it's cracked up to be.

No-one would ever think that Tim Culver's healthy, spent, virile young body could ever have had anything to do with an old witch like Martha Grace. As the whole town knows, the fat bitch is a dyke anyway.

A season or two later and Martha Grace is herself again. Back to where she was before Tim Culver. Back to who she was before Tim Culver. Lives alone, speaks rarely to strangers, pleases only herself. Pleasures only herself. And lives happily enough most of the time. Remembering to cry only when she recalls a time that once reached beyond enough.

FROM THE RIVER'S MOUTH

Sorry luv, don't do south.

No darlin' can't go south of the river this time of night.

South? Over there? Need a passport don't you?

South, no not me, I don't go south, can't go south, won't go south.

Enough. I have heard enough. I have had enough. There is time and there is tide and there is the Thames. Here is the Thames. Old Father Thames they used to say. Because they didn't know any better. Don't know any better. I am no more father than I am mother. But I do have my children, my tributary babies, running into me, clinging to me, come deep down far to me, my Effra and my Peck and my fast fecund Fleet.

I have grown tired of these people who are frightened of water, worried by the south. I am irritated by their gibes, their dismissals, their lack of courage in the face of bridges, tube tunnel terror. Irritation might form a pearl in an oyster shell, but not for me. I twist and I have turned for your pleasure, writhing through your dogged isles and yet you cannot bear to cross me, too scared to cross me? Don't cross me then. Don't you dare cross me. I have had enough. I am very very cross indeed.

I am so old and yet, twice a day, am remade, brand new, flowing through. I have been burned and iced, open and closed, fresh and fetid. You care, I don't. I am not interested in how many species live in me, what is the sand and silt content of my shore, where you would place another rail bridge, road tunnel, ferry landing. I am not interested in land. I am what lies between and I hear the lies you tell one another. Your tube delays and trains cancelled and walking in rain excuses, your getting lost in the south, tossed in the south. All your reasons for not getting there, for being late, for being last. I will not hear excuses any more.

I love my north and my south sides equally. Would you ask me to care more for one than the other? Love one half of me more than the other? And yet you do. You do. Elizabeth flowed from Westminster to Greenwich in my soft arms, Churchill rode me dead in a barge and all the cranes of the city bowed down when he passed. When I was young they carved a version of my face and set me fast on the Cutty Sark's prow, it was like me, but not me. Not quite. I do not allow full likeness and graven images are quickly eroded in water. Cleopatra loaned me a needle once, I was darning something, a sock, a city, I forget which now, I kept her needle, she didn't much care for sewing anyway, was never one for handicrafts, that girl. More makeup than make do and mend. I have been a silver ribbon misleading bombers from Tilbury to Teddington, I have welcomed the Boudicca's flowing blood, I have sat cold and uninterested while the city burned, several times, at my sides.

I have been so much, am so much, and you can't be bothered to cross? I've allowed you a dozen different bridges within an hour's walk. Ferries and ferrymen, water wings and cata-maran. Fine then. I am tired of arguing. You have turned me down once too often. Enough is enough.

Come down here, found here, twist and coiled round here, here I am, silted and salty and waiting. Waiting. The Greenwich Foot Tunnel was opened in 1902. It is fifty feet deep, twelve hundred and seventeen feet long, and it never closes. It runs through me. And I through it, though the white-glazed tiles and dry floor would convince you otherwise. But come closer, it's all right, I won't bite. There. Feel these tiles, smooth and cold, now this one here, see? There is a hook on the wall above you, an old metal hook, rusted just a little through the water in the air, there is always water in the air – touch and look and yes, this tile slips back, and that, and another. Now, quickly, while the lift doors are closed, the camera turned away, reach in and under, and stretch your fingers just that little bit further. That switch, there. Flick it, click it. Ah – and here we are – our entrance hall, a polished-shell path cleared for you. Come in. It's all right, I'm with you now. You do not need to leave a trail of pebbles or crusts. I will bring you back here. I promise. I'm good like that. I always return.

Welcome. Those many man-made bridges? They run over me. The world-renowned tube passes under. But this tunnel, this one tunnel, it passes through. Is passing through. My guests do not pass through. Would you like to meet them? They'd love to meet you. They see so many faces down here. But very few who really know, who come and go.

This is Charlie. He has been here since 1913. Hush now dear, don't cry for the people, it isn't nice to make so much noise, hush, hush . . . I said, shut up! Thank you. Good boy. Charlie was perfectly happy to see young Mary from Bermondsey, as long as she made all the running. Mary walked under the river to the Isle for her tea, a strong cuppa and a nice currant bun, with a kiss and a peck for afters. She caught a ferry to meet him, then walked up to Victoria Park, by the bandstand in the dark where no-one would see his kisses, stolen from her lips. Poor tired Mary stood an hour on the tram all the way to Hampstead for the fair, her one afternoon off and again she journeyed to the far north all for him. Once, just once, Mary asked, couldn't Charlie come to her, bend a little, bend over the water. And then he laughed, right in her face, laughed and shook his head and belched a vulgar grin, his voice raised just that much too loud, his mouth open a little too far, and his words caught on a wind that bore them to me.

'Cross the river? Not me, no fear, you won't catch me crossing there!'

But I did, didn't I, sweetheart? Catch you, caught you, kept you, keep you. Mary cried once or twice, wondered where he'd gone, her daring beau, the darling boy. Then she moved on. Charlie did not move on. Charlie stayed down here with me. Forever nineteen, and never crossing the river, never quite to the other side. His brothers looked up and down the shore for his body, night following night for seven weeks. It never turned up. Because Charlie did not drown. My guests do not drown, they are cool and dry and going nowhere. Ever again. Still, it could have been worse. He could have gone with his brothers to the Somme.

This is Emma. Say hello poppet. Emma? Be nice now, say hello – I mean it. You know what I can do. Say . . . Good.

Thank you. Emma used to work in the City, didn't you, my lovely? Smart job, smart house, smart suit, smart girl. Not so smart girl. All they wanted was one quick trip, that's all they were asking, her friends. A hen night. In Clapham. How bad could it be? But oh no, not our Emma. She just laughed. Laughed in the bride-to-be's face. Giggled behind the back of the long-suffering bridesmaid. Said she'd do her best, see what she could arrange, try, give it a try. Try my eye. She never had any intention of crossing. Not going to chance getting her peep-toes wet, that one. Never had, never would. That was her vow. Proud of it too, she was. Too damn proud. Still, I was patient. I'm happy to wait. I have all my life to flow downstream. And now I have all of Emma's life. My little Queen of the Slip-Tide. How did I catch her if she didn't cross? Good question. See how I bend, I twist? You can barely tell which side I'm on down there at Canary Wharf. And City girls always have to go to the wharf. They're drawn to the bars, the waterfront cafes, the rich, rich men. Ordered steak frites and not a single frite passed her lips. Girl. Emma left her City friends drinking by the water, drinking no water, and went for a wander. Well, I spin into the docks too you know, all those glass-fronted places reflecting my glory, refracting my shadowed light. A wind leapt from the water, splashed single drops on to each of her five hundred pound shoes, Emma bent down to check the leather and then I was there. Now she is here.

Aaron was a taxi driver. He wouldn't go south of the river, not for twenty quid extra, not for a generous tip to the charity of his choice, not for love nor money. He does not go south now either. As I do, he simply leans from east to west and back again on the rising and falling tides. He goes nowhere. An idle man, he would happily sit in his cab, eating bacon sandwiches and drinking large mugs of sweet tea, prefer that to driving south, rather earn less than cross the water, no matter how often his wife reminded him of the bills and the long hours she worked and the mounting debts and the cost of their children's future. Their long fatherless future. Aaron would drive anywhere now if I let him, anywhere at all, his hands hunger for a steering wheel. I won't let him.

Martin travelled all the way from South Africa to London, such a distance he came. But when he got here, the river was one step too many for him. Would only live north, work east, play west. So very impolite. I will not be crossed. Martin's return ticket remains unused and he only remembers the sun. Sam journeyed south from Hexham. Stoke Newington became his new north east, and I the Thames barrier he could not face. Now Sam is my angel of the north and, try as he might, he cannot stretch his arms wide enough to reach the shore. Kane from New Zealand. Feared walking across Hungerford Bridge, mocked what he called my dirty waters, but he needed a closer look to prove London pollution and Antipodean superiority. He got his closer look. Now Kane knows the water all too well, the taste and texture is all he knows, has become expert in the ways of silt and silence, sand blocking his sighs.

There they all are, so many, so much, so missed. So mine.

Anyway, thank you, you should go now. Really, you should go. The tide is turning, London's burning, and you don't want to be down here when it does. Seriously, I mean it. go now. This way, back through here, that's it, past the cool white tiles, bye bye my little ones, I'll be back later, always back later, hush now – hush damn you! Hush! Come on, keep up, don't you want to go back up? To the day and the bright, the riverside light? Didn't you have an appointment? At the Elephant was it? Or Kennington? Putney? You did mean to cross didn't you? Yes? Well go on then, cross. Quick. Off you go. Trip trap over the bridge. Wave good bye. Bye bye. See you again. Maybe. When the moon hangs fat and full over St Paul's and you look down from Waterloo Bridge and you could swear, just swear, there was something in there. Beneath the water. Something, someone. Looking up. Calling out. Asking you to reach in and help. Calling you down. Don't look down. Don't come in. Keep on, cross over, make like the geese, head south. And don't you dare, even in jest, say no to the river crossing. As I said, I'm bored with it. I have had enough. Cross me. Come on. Cross me. I'm waiting.

EVERYTHING IS MOVING,
EVERYTHING IS JOINED

LEWIN MINKOWSKI AND Rachel Taubmann were married beneath the chuppah in the small, light synagogue. Rachel, fully veiled (though Lewin had seen her face already, checked in the ante-room that she was the bride she promised to be, not a substitute ugly stepsister), walked seven times around her bridegroom, the glass was smashed beneath Lewin's foot, they were married. Mr and Mrs Minkowski. Two people, one name.

We were married my love, remember? We smashed glasses when we cheered our union too forcefully, smashed teeth, bones, body, when we came together not too forcefully, but just forcefully enough. Two into one, two as one.

Lewin and Rachel Minkowski came together and out of the shards of broken glass, away from Germany where they themselves had begun, Mr and Mrs Minkowski began their sons. Oskar was born in 1858, Hermann a long, wanted, waiting time later in 1864. He was a summer baby, born the same year that the Governor General of Vilna, according to the wishes of the Tsar, ordered that all school books be printed only in the Cyrillic alphabet, the banning of the Lithuanian language had begun.

In Cyrillic, letters have numerical values, A equals 1, B equals 2; words and numbers are joined.

In 1872, when Hermann was eight years old, one of the works of fiction that later morphed into part of the infamous Protocols of Zion was first translated into Russian and appeared in St Petersburg; several different fictional works, combining, uniting, presenting as one truth. This was also the year that the Minkowski family returned to Germany, Lewin and Rachel's homeland.

Then. There. Hermann was eight, Oskar was fourteen. They were in Königsberg, Prussia. It was 1872. It was not yet Germany. It would be.

Here. Now.

Because the earth is always in motion, because the earth moves around the sun, because the sun moves in the galaxy, the galaxy in the universe and on and on – and in and in, because the thing, anything, you, me, an apple, is made of atoms, is made of electrons, is made of so much we have yet to know – because everything is moving, there is no true co-ordinate for here. Because time is also moving there is no true coordinate for now. We cannot measure here and now because we cannot name the one place to begin our calculation, to say let's start here.

We started here.

And yet we like to think we can do this naming, name the moment, that one point of realisation, of understanding, of love. We like to play with this/now and that/then, and we make plans and determine and build on what is always moving, as if it is stationary, as if it will not change. It's all about perception.

I built on what is always moving when I said yes to loving you.

As a boy, Hermann's mathematical aptitude was noticed at the Gymnasium in Königsberg, he started university in the city in 1880 and also studied at the University of Berlin in the winter that bled from 1882 to 1883. It was during that winter the first permanent street lighting was installed in Leipziger Strasse and Potsdamer Platz. Warm electric light for the cold winter nights of Hermann Minkowski's studies.

Albert Einstein was born in Germany in 1879. His family were secular Jews. His father's name was Hermann. His father worked for a company manufacturing electronic equipment.

Everything is moving, everything is joined.

An apple falls from a tree. In the foreground a train travels along a track. In the distance another train, on a parallel track, travels in the same direction. The apple tree is located between both trains. From the train in the foreground it appears that the train in the background is stationary, that it is the tree that is moving, the tree and the falling apple receding, travelling away, travelling back, behind, travelling to where we've been. It's all about perception.

The trains are moving forward in time and in space. An apple has fallen. The trains have passed on. Past? Present.

You love me. Past.

An apple falls from a tree. I give it to you. Present.

In 1883, the French Academy of Sciences awarded the mathematics Grand Prix to both the nineteen-year-old Hermann

Minkowski for his manuscript on the theory of quadratic forms and also to Henry Smith, an Irish mathematician who would have been fifty-six, had he not died two months before. The time and the place were good for Minkowski, the timing less so for Smith.

An apple falls from a tree. A man is near that tree. From the first train the man on the ground appears to walk slowly, while on the ground the man perceives himself to be walking quickly. If the train is heading east, the apple tree appears to be heading west at an equivalent speed. Close up the apple tree appears stationary. Nothing is stationary, it is all moving. Both move in reality and in time, it's all about perception. Light is the only constant. See? C. Let there be light. Let c be light.

Hermann Minkowski and David Hilbert became friends at university in Königsberg.

We were friends and then we were lovers. I was married to you, became related to you, our wedding day was an event in space and time, but the only constant is the speed of light in a vacuum, and I was not fast enough to keep up with the bright light of you. Our life was no vacuum.

When Minkowski applied for a job at the University of Bonn, his interview was an oral explanation of a paper on positive definite quadratic forms. He got the job. Years later, this oral presentation became the basis of his ideas on the geometry of numbers. And there is a geometry to love, an equation that is always the same.

(Without, with, with, with.)

(With, without, without, without.)

Back to the trains. The trees alongside the track appear to be passing the east-bound train incredibly fast, they go by in a blur, a distant cow, lumbering slowly, ever so slowly, in the opposite direction, appears stationary. But when the train stops, the cow is moving, the tree stationary. Time passes.

Two clocks. One stationary, one moving. The passage of time appears to slow down for the moving clock.

A thirty-year-old man on earth ages a day. A thirty-year-old woman, with the exact birthday as the man, in the (nonexistent) spaceship travelling at light speed also ages a day. Individually, time is a constant for both people. Separately, the man on earth and the woman in space are now different ages. Time for each has passed in the same way. Relative time – his to hers, hers to his – has not.

A thirty-year-old man loves a thirty-year-old woman. She loves him. Love is a constant for both people. His love for her, her love for him, these things are not constant. It's all about perception.

There is space and there is time. Had we world enough and time. We do. And we don't. Relatively speaking. It's all about perception. And an apple falling not mattering as much as it once did. And time passing.

In 1902, Hermann Minkowski, having taught in Zurich (where Karl Jung gained his PhD that same year), and in Königsberg (where Kant held the chair of metaphysics and mathematician Leonard Euler's work led to graph theory) and in Bonn (where Beethoven was born) returned with his family to Göttingen – where the goose girl is kissed by graduating students. David Hilbert had created a position for him in the mathematics department. The old friends, once more in the same time and place, began working together.

I located you, in time, in space. We were once an event, we came together at that place-space – in that time. There are two ways of looking at us, the event of us.

There is this way: With, without, without, without.

And there is this way: Without, with, with, with.

I am time-travelling.

Forward, forward, forward, away from you.

In 1905, Albert Einstein, the theoretical physicist, working in the patent office in Bern, introduced the theory of special relativity in a paper he published on the electrodynamics of moving bodies. Six hundred and forty seven kilometres to the north-north-east, Minkowski and Hilbert were working on mathematical physics, Minkowski particularly interested in the simplicity of equations, the elegance of mathematics.

David Hilbert said of this time, working with his friend, 'Our science, which we loved above all else, brought us together; it seemed to us a garden, full of flowers. In it, we enjoyed looking for hidden pathways and discovered many a new perspective that appealed to our sense of beauty.'

There is no moment. No eureka moment. No overflowing bath, no hypotenuse to square, no apple falling. There is just time. And space. And it was noticed, noted, united. Made a moment and another moment and another moment. Time. A moment of time. A moment of time and space, four – not three – points, to measure all points.

Hermann Minkowski and David Hilbert walk through a

garden together. They look at the flowers, a train goes by. A man in the train sees that Minkowski and Hilbert appear to be passing him. The garden (if it could see) would see both the train and Minkowski and Hilbert moving. The train (if it could see) would see the train tracks as moving. The train tracks (if they could see) see the train and the men pass by. And what do the flowers see? The flowers that are the ideas in the garden of science? They see time.

Herman Minkowski is a mathematician. He wants the equation that makes sense of what is. And what is, is that space and time are linked. Have always been linked. It's just that Minkowski sees this. It's all about perception.

There is this way to write it: (+, -, -, -)

And there is this way: (-, +, +, +).

Length, breadth, depth – and time. Together. Spacetime. Simple. Revolutionary. Quiet.

Mr Newton's law believed it could be possible, if we travelled fast enough, to catch up with a beam of light, with a point in that beam. Mr Maxwell's law of electromagnetism told us we can't, that point of light is travelling at a constant speed away from us, always away. And then Mr Einstein's special relativity found a way through the problem – time and space are not immutable concepts, identically experienced by everyone. In special relativity, time and space become mutable ideas, their appearance and form depending on the observer's state of motion.

A man travels at ten miles an hour is irrelevant unless we know what he is travelling past, from, toward. Simone de Beauvoir quoted Goethe, 'I love you, is it any of your concern?' Lennon and McCartney wrote, 'She loves you'. Yeah yeah.

Yeah. 'I love' is irrelevant unless we know who or what is loved. You were loved. Are loved. Light travels at six hundred and seventy million miles an hour whether anyone is watching or measuring or not, regardless of where from or where to. I love, regardless of you.

Hermann Minkowski and David Hilbert are walking in a flower garden in Göttingen in 1905. It is a sunny day, probably. It is perhaps 11 am. Maybe they are taking a break from thinking about mathematical physics, maybe they are talking about their wives or their children or their jobs, the business of academia, maybe they are not talking about science at all. Maybe they will soon stop walking and sit for *kaffee und kuchen*. They have been friends and colleagues since they were undergraduates in Königsberg, they know each other well. Maybe Hermann Minkowski is thinking he might buy some flowers for his wife Auguste, maybe he is pondering the geometry of numbers. Certainly the flowers have their own geometry.

Perhaps the garden is 20 metres from the university office. Maybe the garden is quite small, only 100 metres by 100 metres. Maybe it is spring, there are plants, but they are not yet fully-grown, somewhere between ten and one hundred centimetres above the earth. Some of them will become bigger – higher, wider, deeper – in time.

It is 11.10 am. It is time to leave the garden and go back to work, away from the work that is the discussion of ideas in the garden to the work that is the discussion of ideas inside. Different spaces, same work.

It is time to leave this time and space and go on to another time and space, inside the building. Maybe Hermann Minkowski, walking in a flower garden, in Göttingen, Germany, with his friend and colleague David Hilbert, understands, as he checks his watch, that time has passed as they walked in this garden. Maybe the mathematician Hermann Minkowski, who taught courses attended by the young Albert Einstein, is thinking of Euclidean geometry – the measuring of space, of things in space – and maybe Hermann Minkowski, who has been married to Auguste Adler for eight years, and is the father of two young daughters, Lily who is seven, and Ruth who is three, maybe, this German Jew who was born in Russia a quarter century before Adolf Hitler, who is walking with David Hilbert just four years before he himself will die at only forty-four of a sudden appendicitis, maybe Hermann realises, looking at the time that has passed, in this garden, with his friend with whom he talks about ideas, that young Albert Einstein's theory of special relativity can be easier explained – far more simply, cleanly, beautifully explained – if time and space (11.13 am, the flower garden, outside his office in Göttingen, Germany) are considered together. The three dimensions of space, and the one of time, four dimensions as one. Spacetime.

In 1908, Hermann Minkowski wrote a new paper and gave a speech to the Assembly of German Natural Scientists and Physicians. It was their eightieth such assembly. Minkowski explained that the work of Lorentz and Poincaré, which in turn led to Einstein's special relativity, could be better understood, more clearly, more elegantly, by bringing time to space and space to time. By taking the three dimensions of space and adding the fourth that is time.

And with spacetime, the (relatively) young Albert Einstein developed the general theory of relativity.

In 1909 Hermann Minkowski died of a ruptured appendix. He was forty-four.

Here's a thing: before spacetime, before Einstein and Minkowski and Lorentz and Poincaré, and all the others, before them, back when, back then, with Newton, we believed gravity was all. We believed it held us, elliptically, to the sun. We believed that if the sun were to collapse in on itself, to explode, to otherwise die, then we too, our planet, this little earth, that we here would be simultaneously – at the same time – thrown out, thrown off course, away forever. (Or in forever, forever in.) Now we know better, we know that it takes eight minutes for the light of the sun to reach us. Eight minutes for that light, travelling at light speed, to find our earth. The sun could die and we would only find out eight minutes later, when the light failed. It might feel as if we found out at the same time as it happened, because we wouldn't know it had happened until we saw it, but it would already have happened.

I didn't know you had gone until long after the fact, I didn't know you had left me until I saw the evidence – you, the body of you, the cold, waxy body of you. You had, of course, left much earlier. We always do.

We are not held by gravity to the sun, we are held in gravity, in the warp and weft of it, with the sun. Not to or from but with. Not one and the other, but together. And if that sun, our sun, fell, collapsed, exploded, imploded, died, it would be the ripple of that disturbed, rolling, roiling weft we felt as much as the absence of light.

I feel the absence of you. I feel the loss of you as much as I see that you are not here. Like those who first understood spacetime, I know our gravity is much bigger than just the pull of me to you, you to me. It surrounds me and holds me up, over, under, in. It holds me through and through. Without you, I am not held.

Hermann Minkowski said, 'Henceforth space by itself, and time by itself, are doomed to fade away into mere shadows, and only a kind of union of the two will preserve an independent reality.'

Two meaning far more as one than as their separate two. Two mattering far more together than apart. Two as one to make sense of both two and of one.

I am a shadow and there is no light to make me.

There is a Buddhist concept, *esho funi,* it translates as 'two but not two, one but not one'. That's spacetime my love, that was us. And in time, because of time, because neither space nor time can ever part again – it is us still.

Everything is moving, everything is joined. It's all about perception.

NO

THEY PLAY LOUD Japanese music. It is modern, as they are. Modern and strange to the western ear. Quite possibly strange to the Japanese ear too – this music is avant garde. Whatever the Japanese for the French is. The chants slam and swing blind metallic through their perfect house, across the raked gravel garden and batter at the neighbours' imperfect doors. Theirs is all ideal home, house and garden minimalist white and they are the black cloaked maximum therein.

The playing is loud in their residential haven. It is foreign and abstract and penetrates past language and known forms and far into that place where even too loud is not loud enough. It is more than welcome. It brings her back to within herself, to what she once was. These days she sees him and her, sees the we, as he and she too often. Too often for her own comfort, for his own desire. She would not be separate if at all possible. Music plays and they are serious and newly important and self respecting in their intake of too strong black coffee and not enough cocaine and barely sufficient slow aged island whiskey. They have perfumed skin and hair and mouths and wear foolishly expensive designer clothes in many shades of black. They pose on cold bridges in London and dark alleys in other cities and then they catch themselves and laugh at the lunacy of the pose. But strike it anyway.

She is thin and he is thinner, but she has reasons for her greater mass. The perfect creation excuse for the thin band of narrow flesh that encapsulates her once vicious hips, her clawing bones. The fresh flesh will go though, sooner than it came. She will see to that. She has no further need of padding.

He and me a unit, just the two of us inseparable and nothing could come between us. Until now. Now that this small screaming thing has come between our comings. It cries through the night through the day. It is mewling and puking and we did not want it, could not envisage this and we are trying to get at the truth but do not know where it is hidden. We ask the questions but no-one can answer us honestly now. Do you like yours or do you not? The inquiry is direct and basic but the answers will not come. We ask, is this normal? The distance that we feel? But the old ladies nod their parkinsonian heads and goo and gah and lad fathers are now new men who delight in their ability to reveal softness and swim in glee that this fresh self exposure is a medal-worthy activity at the pub and even the mature mothers, not young but new all the same, coo and consort in the terrible room of labour comparisons. And so we are left bereft because no-one will talk to us of the truth. We are obviously wicked. We are obviously bad parents. We are obviously bad.

It's not that they don't love the child. It was not accidental, they did decide to admit it into their lives. Conscious choice not taken lightly. They simply love each other rather more. The music is intense. It rockets back from the sitting room through expensively non-reverberating speakers and along finely polished floorboards into the kitchen the bedroom the bathroom where they hide from the wailing infant, the smiling infant, in the stark and cool white room at the end of the hall. The long hours sanding floorboards that were not intended for softest knees, edible baby flesh dancing across the glistening boards. There are gongs and chimes and then dead silence followed by other percussive accents they have no names for. There is extremity of sound and without vision she does not know what he is listening to, he cannot picture her mind's eye. But they try. There is silence and un-pattern and howling, noises from the ether that at the same moment are also so very earth. There is simply sound and she can kiss him and he can hold her and they are lovers in the bed of resonance.

I love him. I have always loved him. The hour we met knew I had always loved him, my skin flayed itself from my bones, leaping out to touch him, the fine thin lines and man in black drawn sharp across my field of vision, ready to take me in take me up make me up other woman another location to that place where I was only his always his, the palace of bliss.

His yielding was equally whole, his dismissal of the self for the two made one, just as total. They chose in that instant at that dinner party in that fat London suburb to belong. They did not get around to mentioning their truth for another four weeks. It didn't matter. The promise of always had already been made, vowed in complicity when first their eyes met over a proffered smoked salmon canapé, glistening caviar sprinkled. They refused, politely. They are vegetarian.

I saw her and fell fast into her, fell diving, fell as intentional leap, fell because if I did not fall I would regret forever and not know why not and never be again. And anyway, I had no choice. I gave myself without reservation and without any possibility of redemption. There was only her, is only her and I am slave to that, master of this. She is my definite article.

Your whisky is too good. It deadens the senses I have just woken with cocaine. Now you are offering grass. What is this, Salome? A den of iniquity or a nursery? I am full of you, wish woman, and yet you are so fine already, a thin copy of the mother of our child, you are whittling away at yourself, returning your fecund round to my matching thin. I applaud your willpower, your strength of desire. The world marvels at your fine mother's breasts and stick thin figure. Your impaler's hips are coveted specimens. You clever little thing, you.

Certainly this drugs and alcohol diet works well. I am already back to myself. Back to ourselves. We are nearly us again.

And still the child screams. Or perhaps it wakes and smiles. Coos, giggles tries new words and turns its head. It is a glamour child of catalogue proportions and advertising bright features. It is a gold mine and a delight. And when it cries again as inevitably it will, it is held, touched gently, lovingly, reverentially. Is kissed and bathed and adored because it is perfect and they are so clever to have made this between them.

And that my darling is the problem. There is absolutely nothing wrong with this child, except that it is the held grace note, unnecessary between us. You are tired and have no time for me and I am tired and have no eyes to see the pain in yours, because I am sleeping and only in that sleep is there a space to realise what we both know. This cannot go on.

You whisper it to me in dreams and I am so afraid of what you are saying and so equally delighted that you say it. You braille the suggestion on my back, naked and tattooed and yearning, and I am delighted to hear you think so too.

And how can we, how could we, runs on and on. This child is defenceless and adorable and makes the right noises and is beginning to learn mama and papa. We could let this all continue, we could make it possible to be three instead of two in one. We could try couldn't we?

Well yes, I suppose we could, but fuck it you are mine and I want all of you all that you are. It sucks at your breasts, they that are my breasts for my touch and if that child was someone else some adult else I would break every finger slowly and with deliberate ease for the touch with which it caresses you. Instead I kiss it and soothe it and lay you down to sleep and return to lay you down for real, but you are laid out prostrate with motherhood and I am worn down by fatherhood and we drift holding hands into the fitful sleep that is our promise for the next five, ten, fifteen, twenty-five, thirty-five, forty-five years. The half sleep of the parent ever listening for the call from the child.

We play louder music now and still the dream chimes and ecstatic cries do not drown out our child. We have found another composer and another, they are getting harder to listen to, these avant garde men and their fields of furrowed noise. We take in whole albums at a time now, I cannot leave the room for fear of missing the nuance the subtlety the accusation that wipes away your face and turns you from cool perfection into gibbering wreck of tidal sound weave. The walls make tsunami of this music. I am listening hard for the way out. Then you tell me it is found.

She does not believe him. Does not really think that he will take this ultimate step. And yet she has never doubted him before. Has always taken his every word as gospel. But even the gospels are contradictory, Matthew and Mark were not really good friends and only John loved Mary.

The rain falls still but a gravel garden has no need of gratitude.

I am Martha not Mary and prepare supper. We eat together – a narrow bar of thin dark chocolate, more than 70% cocoa solids stretched between four quivering lips. The child talks to itself, sweetly gurgling. We close the door. This moment needs privacy. Our second course is liquid, I take the single malt, he reaches for the sluggish vodka, hot and bitter pepper frozen into the empty liquid. Now we are 110% proof. We play music ever louder and float into a Zen garden of he and me, his fingers rake the white gravel of my skin and he soothes my whiskey burnt mouth with his cool tongue. Then we turn to dessert.

The long lines of coke snake towards us, I am the mongoose reversed and spellbound before the line you lay out for me across your concave chest. I empty my lungs for greater depth, wait until the last possible moment when diaphragm is beating syncopated against my ribs, begging for air. I bend to your thin man torso and breathe in coke and you and the drug is unheeded, unnecessary. It is you that rushes straight to my brain, you are the amphetamine lift quickening my heart and you are far inside me.

I leave her, spinning in the euphoria of potential, turn volume up to the last notch before I go, this is no time to worry about what the neighbours think. She is sitting on the floor, bare boards and bare body, light white room and only sound.

The chimes turn through intermittent silences into a moan into a wail, soon the wail will rise to screams and then, in the white noise of action, the task will be masked. I bless her shut eyes face and close the door quietly behind me. In the hall is a stillness, a waiting. Now it is done.

I listen only to the music, I hear only the screams from the speakers, I understand only the wailing created through improvised electronic no-pattern and interpreted by my shivering flesh. My senses are confused with the alcohol/amphetamine mix, my body does not know whether to accept the depressant or run with the energiser, it sits in limbo while sound washes across me, wailing and screaming, discordant gongs and perfect chimes breaking free, drowning out every other tone in the house. I flow through the sound for an exact eighty six minutes and then, in the white room through the white halls in the white house, there is silence. It creeps up on me as memory of winter. There is silence and now there will be peace. I rise and on shaking legs go to thank him, anoint his courage.

In the corner of an almost empty white room, a pale cradle sits. It is quiet and the woman walks unsteadily to it. Walks slowly to kiss the stopped child. And then halts. The child lies eyes wide and smiling. The child breathes and smells sweet baby. The woman is first angry and then immediately relieved and grateful and pacified and picks up the child and holds him close to her. Kisses his soft head and listens as his breath falls against her assaulted ear. She turns again for the door, cradling the child, turns for her partner. Then she sees him, half hidden behind the open door, wet red glossy against white walls. Sees him and hears again the cries she ignored beneath the music, the wailing and the moaning, the screams and the long, dying lament.

He is the avant guard. He has saved me.

The child begins to whimper and she holds it to her breast and kisses the blood red lips of the other and feeds the child and drinks from the man and is grateful, very grateful, not to have to choose ever again.

LADIES' FINGERS

She points at me again. The finger is swollen at both joints. She lies in the bed, cannot move or speak. Points. Just her left hand, heavy with an unfulfilled engagement ring. Points from me to the bed. Smooth bed, cool bed, pillow-decked and silent. This room used to be a whole, now it is the lesser sum of many parts. I cross the room, twelve halting steps, drawn and unwilling, I pull back the fine sheet, lift and lay her out. Each limb placed beside the others, all of them in the correct place, still joined, but as useless as if I had severed them singly in the night. As if I would sever them singly in the night.

I take her to the toilet, she shits, pisses, farts. I wipe her like a baby but nothing like a baby she is old and her skin smells. Smells of age and decay. Particular smells. I think some part of her likes these smells. She would call them human scents, real, truthful. If she could speak beyond a croak for air. She points to the window. I gladly let in cool night, take it inside me in thick sips, welcome the smell of wet vegetation from the unloved garden. And immediately she points again. More insistent this time, bony finger grown thinner and longer. I understand (because I am very understanding) and close the window, close the heavy curtain, worn and dusty velvet, fully lined, from before the war. She is calm again, holds the pointing finger at her side, inadequate lungs shiver her thin frame beneath the sheets, she slips into a place near sleep. I sit and wait. Watching for the hand to raise, the finger to point from me to whatever she wants. Age and stupidity and too much fun and three strokes have done this. Reducing her to an old woman with spittle at the corner of her mouth and a nicotine-stained finger.

I dip her into the bath, testing the water first, it is warm and swirls around her, flowing into the crevices left by wrinkled years. The skin folds mark out lines a skilled surgeon might cut along. If she would let them in, let them look at her, let them try. She will not let them in. She believes in time taking its true course. She believes in suffering and in pain. Hers and mine. Her dry dying skin flakes off into the water, she lies in her water, pisses into it, cannot stop herself, does not try. Lies there in her own dead cells and piss. I soap her body, hold her just firm enough, just gentle enough. I am surprisingly considerate for one so angry. Her body teaches me its needs.

In the middle of the night I wake to her pointing. To the finger, ring grown tight around the base, forcing her flesh out and angry dark red against the old gold, rolling in the bed in frustration and impotent fury at my rest. The finger is angry with me. I was meant to be watching. This scene is all for me. I have slept in the old cane chair again and stand, gently sliding muscles against tendon and bone. I stretch my limbs, almost unconscious of her seething jealousy at my abundant mobility. Almost. But as she calms her rage enough to watch me through watery eyes, I choose to stretch just that little more, push my bones against the limits of their skin barriers, to scratch my arse with just that slightly louder sigh of satisfaction. It is

48

better while she sleeps. Easier to study the failing body, easier to sneak in just a little night air. She tries a croaking of saliva in the back of her throat, but in her anger becomes confused and grows silent again while she tries to remember whether to inhale or swallow what is in her decaying mouth. I want her to shut up. I want to shut her up. I want to shut her in. Leave this tight room, walk out into the world. Return to the street with yellow lamplight and cold wind and the possibility of rain to wash every piece of her out of my head.

Instead I stand. Stretch. Walk. My movements are as deliberate as her pointing finger. She points at the book. I pick it up, sit closer to the burning light, turn the dry page. In fifty six minutes she is asleep again and my throat is hoarse. I pick up her water glass, wipe her dark lipstick stain from the edge and sip. The water is warm and smells of her kiss, I gag but force it down. I return to my chair and the list of remembrances. A beach at sunset. A full fridge, every item neatly labelled. Running to catch a bus. Lying awake in a daylight bed and feeling the charge of could-be desire as it lies beside me. Freesias stolen from a neighbour's garden. Cold toast, dry, crisp. A burning hot shower raining down my back, counting each knuckled vertebra as it falls, quickly turning the tap to cold just for the effect it has on my nipples. I think of my sex then and my hand steals to me. From outside my clothes I stroke myself, against the line of this skirt, these stockings, against the grain I stroke myself, come close to me again, my eyelids begin their wanting flutter and I half focus on the bed. She is watching. I start up, a five year old caught stealing sweets, and run to slap her face. She still smiles, straining thin muscles to curve her desiccated lips into a half moon, rictus smile with the pointing finger curling towards me, sniffs appreciatively and then gaping grins once more. I hit her again. My slapping hand is as much my own as her pointing finger, as ill controlled. She tries to laugh but it comes out in a thin gurgle, catching on her windpipe and throttling her. Laughter choking her laugh.

I should sit her up, help her to breathe, she points at me, she is not laughing now, she is fighting for her breath, fighting me for her breath. Still pointing, the ring heavy, dragging her hand down to the counterpane, the stains dark, the nail overgrown, twisted and yellowing. Her lips are blue. There is no other blue in this room. How interesting I should note the lack of blue. Then. Now. She points again, at the window, the night, the cool wet air, points from me to herself. Again. Bloody pointing finger. I understand, how could I not? But I do not answer. I stand above her wriggling body, watching the spasms jolt around her tired organs. This will not do her any good, she will bruise inside, a brittle egg carton holding cracked goods. There there little heart, hush sweet liver, come now my darling kidney. And then, quite suddenly, the only thing moving is the finger on the end of her hand. She gasps. It is the widest she has opened her mouth in three months. I see her rotting molars. Her involuntary diaphragm snaps itself back again and again, forcing her gaping mouth to suck and gasp, she flares her nostrils, straining to drag in the air she has insisted I shut out. It is no good. The blue stretches from lips to face to eyes, heavenly blue now, and empty.

I breath then myself. I had not known I was holding my breath, waiting, anticipating. With twelve slow steps I return to my chair. Sit, rest, sleep. Easily and full. This is the first good night's sleep I have had in many months. I am so tired.

It is weeks over. The earth starts to settle over her clean and catalogued body. The morning after I wrenched the curtains from their poles and now I keep the windows open to let in the night until the chill is damp and heavy in the centre of the room. After I had cleaned her, labelled her insides, they took her away in a narrow coffin, lined like the curtains with thin red silk. They dug a deep hole, laid her down and smothered the body, the only gasping against black loam. It was all done. She was all done.

Now, even her finger is still. I know. I kept it. Sitting in the bottom of my carryall. Ring still heavy on the finger, stains still yellow. In the quiet of my wide-windowed night I open the box and take out the pointing finger. I point at things in the room and laugh. It is not so fierce. It is just a finger. Pointing at just a liver. Just a kidney. Just a heart. Just the finger of my lover. The woman I adored. She who I loved and caressed and cared for and hated and allowed to die. The woman who surrendered to her own inner decay. She who schooled me in the individuality of body parts. Who taught me to see a hundred shining units in one composite flesh. I hold her pointing finger. And in a soft box of palest cotton wool the nail still grows, yellow, curled. It points to my heart. And I wait in the night, sit patient in my chair, until the moment it pierces me. Soon.

UN BON REPAS DOIT
COMMENCER PAR
LA FAIM . . .

THE JOURNEY FROM London to Paris is easy. Too easy. I need more time, to think, prepare, get ready. Security, supposed to be so important now, these days, ways, places, is lax to the point of ease. I love it, welcome the apparent ease. I believe in fate, in those big red buses lined up to knock us over, in your number being up, the calling in of one's very own pleasure boat. I do not believe that taking off our shoes at airports will save us. I show my ticket and my passport, walk through to the train, and get off at the Gare du Nord. Too easy. Too fast.

Less than three hours after leaving London I walk straight into a picket line. It seems the French staff are less fond of the lax security than I. Or perhaps they just don't like the non-essential immigrants they say Eurostar is employing. I accept the badly-copied leaflet thrust into my hand and put it in my pocket. *Bienvenue en France.*

I can't face the metro. Not yet, this early, it is not yet mid-morning. In real life I would choose to be asleep, safe in bed – not always achieved, but it would be my choice. I like my metro in the afternoon and evening, a warm ride that promises a drink at the other end, a meal maybe, lights. In the morning it is too full of workers and students, those interminable French students, segueing from lycee to university with no change of clothes between. Ten years of the same manners, same behaviour day in day out, week after week of congregating in loud groups on footpaths where they smoke and laugh, and then suddenly they're in the world and somehow those ugly duck student girls are born again as impossibly elegant *Parisiennes*, fine and tidy and so very boring in their classic outfits. French and Italian women, groomed to identical perfection and not an original outfit among them. So much more interesting naked. Round the picket line, out into the street. Road works, illegal taxi drivers offering their insane prices to American tourists just in from London (theatre), Paris (art), Rome (Pope). The Grand Tour as dictated by the History Channel.

I cross the street in front of the station, head down, heading toward the river. There is something about traversing a map from north to south that feels like going downhill, even without the gentle slope from here to the water. Where I'm headed it certainly feels like going downhill. I don't want to look at this city, not now. I see gutters running with water, Paris prides itself on clean streets, on washing every morning, a whore's lick of running cold to sluice out the detritus. Two young women with their hands held out, sit at the edge of businessmen's feet, rattling coins in McDonalds cups. I try to pass but their insistence holds me, I say I don't speak French, they beg again in English. I insist I don't speak that either, they offer German, Italian and Spanish. I have no more words in which to plead either ignorance or parsimony, I scavenge in three pockets before giving them a dollar. It's my only defence against their European polyglossary.

Still too early. Still too soon.

Paris is small. The centre of Paris I mean. Like every other city with a stage-set centre, there are all those very many suburbs, the ones Gigi never saw, where cars burn and mothers weep and it is not heaven accepting gratitude for little girls. It is not heaven I am thanking now. I continue my walking meditation, past innumerable Vietnamese restaurants, and countless small patisseries where pains au chocolat and croissants dry slowly on the plates of high glass counters, and bars serve beers to Antipodean travellers who really cannot believe this city and call home to tell loved ones readying for bed about the pleasures of a beer in a café at ten in the morning. That glass Pyramid can wait, this is art, this is the life.

It is a life. Another one.

There are no secrets. This isn't that kind of story. Nothing to work out. I can explain everything, will explain everything. But not yet. There are things to do and it must be done in order and the thing is, the thing is, we always had lunch first. She and I. She said it was proper, correct. That French thing, their reverence for food, an attitude the rest of the world outwardly respect and secretly despise. It's just food for God's sake, why must they make such a fuss? The linen the glass the crockery the menu the waiters with their insistence on pouring and placing and setting and getting it all right. Pattern, form, nothing deviating, nothing turning away, nothing new. Like the groomed women and the elegant men and the clean, clipped lap dogs. Nothing to surprise. So perhaps more than a reverence for just food, a reverence for reverence, reverence for form. Female form, polite form, good form, true to form. Formidable. Hah. Polyglot that.

(So strange. I can walk down the street, give money to a beggar, I can make a play on word form. I am able to buy a train ticket, sit in a bar, order wine and slowly drink the glass as if nothing has happened, as if life just goes on. Even when I know how very abruptly it can stop.)

So. Lunch. Dinner. From the Old French *disner*, original meaning: breakfast, then lunch, now dinner. Because any attempt to dine, at whatever time of day, will of course, break the fast that has gone before, whatever time period that fast encapsulated, night, morning or afternoon. Whenever I broke my fast with her, for her, she insisted we dine first.

Some time ago I spent a weekend with friends in London. At their apartment, their flat, my London friends talk about words. The English are very good at discussing words, it lessens their power, words as landmines, easily triggered, makes them read-able, understandable. Stable. My friends discussed lunch or dinner, dinner or tea. If the difference were a north/south divide or a class construct. In London they talk about north and south of the river, here it is left and right. The faux-bohemian sinister and the smooth, the neat, the adroit. I prefer north and south, it's harder to get lost. Apparently they've found her. Marie-Claude. Found her body. It's why I'm here.

When I tear my eyes from the gutters and the beggars and the street corners designed to frame a new picture with every stone edge, I look to high chimneys. I am not keen to see shop doors and windows, avenues and vistas, not yet. There is something I need to see first. One thing. I can manage right up and far down, to the far sides, I have the opposite of tunnel vision. There is graffiti, very high, on tall chimneys and cracked walls where one building has been leaning too long on another. This is not what they mean when they talk about a proper view, a scene in every Parisian glance, but it's diverting enough. I am eager to be diverted. I take a left turn and a right one and another left, still closer to the river, nearer the water, but a narrow road uphill now, heading east, there are more people on the street, or less space for them to walk, they touch me sometimes, their clothes, coats, swinging arms. I do not want to be touched, not like this anyway, not dressed, covered, hidden. It will all be open soon.

These side streets, those to the left and the right, east and west, are not as pretty as the views the tourists adore. She and I sat together once, in the restaurant, and listened to an old Australian couple discuss the difference between London and Paris. The woman said Paris was so much prettier, the French had done very well not to put the ugly modern beside the old beautiful. Her husband agreed. And then he said, in a tone calculated to reach the walls of stone, that the French had capitulated during the war. That is why their city was not bombed, why Paris was prettier than London. Though he agreed, the weather was better too, which helped no end. The afternoon progressed, the Australian man drank more wine, and he went on to eat every course the waiters placed before him. I cannot begin to think how much of the waiters' saliva he must also have enjoyed.

The street I find myself in now is not that pretty. It is poor and messy. Here they sell kebabs and Turkish slippers and cigarettes, and the bread in these shops was not freshly baked on the premises first thing this morning, and the fruit has not been raised lovingly in a farmer's field with only sunshine and rain to help it on its way, there are no artisans here. But this is Paris too, regardless of how few tourists see these sights. Marie-Claude showed me these streets, brought me here to explain that there were worlds where no-one cared if the Pyramid was appropriate or not, that the walls around Rodin's garden were too high for locals to climb, that even one euro for a good, fresh, warm croissant is too much for too many. She insisted she knew these streets well and they knew her and that what I read as amused tolerance in the faces of the half-strangers she greeted was friendship and acceptance to her. It may well have been. She is not here now for me to compare the look in her eyes against theirs and I do not have the courage to lock eyes with these men. These shopkeepers are all men. I have thought about this many times. Where are the women shopkeepers? Can they really all be at home with so many children and so much housework and such a lot to do that they do not want to run their own family business, stand alongside their loved one, work hand in hand? Or perhaps they not have the skill to sell all this stuff? These lighters and batteries that will die in a day. These shoes made by God knows how many small children in how many village factories. Perhaps it is simply that women are better with fruit and vegetables, the items that were once, more recently, living. Maybe this is why the women run market stalls while their husbands and sons and fathers run shops. Or perhaps the women are afraid of bricks and mortar, always ready to pick up their goods and run.

She did not like to run, Marie-Claude, said it made her too hot, sticky. Sticky was not good. Cool and calm and smooth and tidy and groomed and perfect. These things were good, right, correct. To be that way, held in, neat, arranged, arrayed, that was appropriate, proper. *Propre*. Which is clean. And it is also own, as in one's own. Thing, possession, person. One word, two meanings. So many ambiguous words. Yes. No. The things that can be read into any phrase. And accent makes a difference of course, culture, upbringing. We often fail to understand those we grew up with, our brothers and sisters, mistaking their yes for no, truth for lies, despair for hope. How much harder to understand total strangers, when they stand at shop doors, form a picket line, love you, leave you, cheat, lie, misbehave.

It was the drugs of course. It always is. She simply couldn't say no, *non*, *nyet*, *nein*, *ne*. That's what I hate about all those heroin chic films – one of the many things I hate about all those heroin chic films – how they always make the users look so dirty. Messy. Unkempt. She, as I have explained, was the opposite. Our media, those stupid cop shows and the angry young men films made by angrier (but so much duller, and often older than they admit) young men, has convinced us that the drugs make you ugly, your hair lank, eyes glazed, skin grey. Which could not be further from the truth in her case, her metabolism loved it, thrived on it. Yes, she might not have been able to keep going at this rate for more than another decade, she'd have had to slow down eventually, but careful, planned use, clean equipment and good veins, hungry lungs, open mouth, eager nose – her body loved it all. Loved all her body. I did. He did. They did. She did. We did. Maybe you did. I don't know, it doesn't matter, this is my side of the story. Yes. Yes. In my own time, taking your time to explain. I apologise, I know you value your time . . .

I do not mean explain as in excuse. I mean as in reason. There are always reasons.

There was the habit of course, the way ex-smokers regret the loss of a packet to open, cellophane to rip off, mouth to hold, match to strike. I know she liked the accoutrements, the little bit of this and little bit of that, the choice of vein, the pick of needles – in her job she had the pick of needles – the choice of drug too of course. For up or down or round and round.

Here it is. He was her husband, is her husband, and I her lover. Then he found out, talked to me, told me some of her other truths, and now she is dead. That's why I'm here, to help with the confirmation. She is drowned, was drowned, has been drowned. Which makes sense. She adored her bath, Marie-Claude, sadistic marquise in soothing warm. The bathroom was her shrine. It was the right place to do it, to stop, in the shrine to herself and her form and her desire. Always her desire. Not for her the current vogue for minimalist white, cool and plain. She chose the palest pale apricots and soft barely-there peaches and tiniest hints of warm flesh to tint her warm room, the warmer shades coloured her own skin tones better. Only very tiny babies look good in white, she once said, it suits their newborn blue, the veins that are not yet filled out with warm blood, blue and white and the clean absence of colour suit only a learner heart, lungs in practice. The rest of us need warmth on our skin, colour in our light. Cold winter mornings were her hardest time. Although that must have been hard too, the night last week, a warm evening and her face held under the water, nose and grasping mouth under the water, until her lungs exploded and she breathed a mermaid's breath just once.

There is a plan here. I have followed it to the letter. His letter.

I go to her restaurant, our restaurant, their restaurant. I

ask for her table. The waiter, clearly a part-timer, one I have not seen before, raises an eyebrow, the maître'd, just turning from seating a couple of regulars, sees me, hurries over. Pushes the foolish young man aside, takes both my hands in his, takes my jacket, takes my arm, takes me. He is so very sorry. I must be tired. Here, here is my seat, here is her table, there are tears in his eyes. They will feed me he says, it will be their pleasure, they are so sorry. I expect they are. She was here almost every day. Not always with me. Of course the staff here are sorry.

I eat my meal. Three courses. I do not need to order, the patron himself tells the waiter to say that this is his recommendation, I agree. The patron does not come to speak with me, not yet, not now. He has work to do, and so do I. And anyway, he and I should not be seen together, not yet. Wine. Water. Coffee. Armagnac. She thought it was very foreign of me to ask for liqueur with my coffee. The kind of thing only tourists or old ladies might do. Apparently it was inelegant, childish. I did it despite her disapproval. I do it to spite her now, despite her now.

A classic French meal, in a classic Paris restaurant. Sun shining through the mottled glass windows, lead light yellow and green and red. A businessman dines alone across from me. He too has three courses and wine and coffee, and will go to the office after his three hour break and work steadily until dark. A wealthy tourist couple argue over the menu, entirely in French, it makes no concession to their cash, demands they rack their misspent youth for lost words. To my right a young couple, run from their work for half an hour here and an hour in bed, then back to run the world. To my left a middle-aged gay couple and their sleeping dog. This is civilised Paris, the dog is as welcome as the homosexuals. Everyone should eat well, taste is all. I could sit here all afternoon and stare around me. I could never go to my next appointment. I have no choice. It is fortunate that the young man who places the burning plate in front of me with a low '*attention madame*' annoys me, draws me back to this place, this time, to what happens next. He annoys me in two ways. One, as he too clearly stated, I am madame, not mademoiselle. He could have been kinder, generosity is always welcome. Two, I didn't think it was just the plate he was suggesting needed care. This I understand as well. Those that fed her knew her. There are many things of which I must be careful.

They are well-trained though, these young men. Young men only of course, no waitresses, the food too precious to be tainted by women's hands. These are the best. There is the waiter who, hearing a lighter fail to strike three times across the room, arrives with another lighter, working correctly. The customer wishes to light his own cigar and the waiter leaves it beside him. Two minutes later, cigar lit and smoking, the customer continues to strike again and again at his own lighter, striking against hope, the failure of his own tool still a problem despite the waiter's speedy solution to the immediate problem. And where any normal person might laugh at the man, or think him a bloated fool, too occupied in his missing flame to pay attention to his charming dinner companion, she who sits bored and irritated by his attention to pointless detail, the waiter senses the man's distress as well as the woman's slow fury, takes away the offending lighter, there is fuel in the kitchen he says, and returns just moments later, the fresh flame a bright torch to lead him on.

I love these windows, in summer they slide back to tables on the street, in winter they hold back, with their coloured glass, the worst of the grey. Today they keep me in warmth, for now. Cheese. Time is passing. Time is near. I feel it, waiting, demanding. I wonder if she felt it, if she knew her time was near. I doubt it. She had such an exquisite sense for food, for wine, for sex, for fabric – a perfect cut, an ideal line. But very little awareness at all of the kind of day to day passing of time that most of us understand once we have left youth behind, once we are madame not mademoiselle. One of the perfectly-trained young men takes a short stout knife and digs me out a crumbling chunk of roquefort. It is not what I asked for. I did not ask. In his wisdom he decided this the correct coda to my meal. It is perfect, both creamy and crystalline, aggressive in my mouth. I also requested goat's cheese. His disdain is too well-trained to show a customer of my long standing. In contrast to the roquefort it is a smooth bland paste. The young man is right, it is no doubt wrong to eat the two together, yet, in my mouth, where they belong, the blend is perfect. The one all flavour and bite, the other a queen of texture, of touch. Marie-Claude and I were no doubt wrong together, actually perfect. No doubt perfect, actually wrong.

Through the hatch at the back of the room, I watch the only black man in the building. Daoud has spent the past hour washing dishes, will give hours yet. Sweat falls in a constant drip from his face to the scalding greasy water, his bare hands plunge repetitively, constant action, disregarded heat, all movement, all moment. I am fond of Daoud, my French is poor, his English non-existent, we have smiled to each other through his hatch, during a hundred or more lunches. I have always thanked him too, for his work. Marie-Claude said that in Algeria he had his own restaurant. She dismissed it though, said the food could not be of any standard. I am not especially fond of north African food myself, often find it cloying, heavy. But Daoud is a generous man and, much as I suspect he found her non-recognition easier to bear than my typical foreign civility to all, he did not repel my need to patronise, to charm. Today he has not once looked towards me. He must know I am here, but he has not offered me a glance. In the time-honoured tradition of silent servants and slaves everywhere, I assume he knows what was done. Or maybe he's just pissed off I haven't been here for so long. I doubt many of the customers here feel enough white liberal guilt to specifically insist that some of the tip must be shared with the dishwasher. I wonder which annoys him more? My need to expiate the colonist's guilt with ten euro notes or my part in the death of his boss's wife? Fortunately I do not speak his languages. He will never be able to tell me.

Near the end of the service the man himself comes out from the kitchen, the patron. A big man, with the haircut he fell in love with at the age of eighteen and hasn't cared to change for forty years, his broad body held into the black shirt and trousers beneath the stained apron, not a traditionally good looking man by any means, but his food is beautiful. His staff must have told him I was here the moment I entered the building, but he has waited until after the meal, as always, to come and be among his guests. He walks the room, greeting customers and friends as if they were all alike. He does not come to my table, to me at her table. I understand. This is a public place, he must be careful. We must be careful.

I drain the last of my armagnac, an oil slick of golden liquid clinging to the side of the glass. I am tempted to run my finger in the residue, lick it up. I don't. I pay my bill, leave the room, I have an appointment near the river.

I leave the restaurant in the quiet street with no river view, full of food and wine and apprehension. I enjoyed the meal, it was always good to eat there, but as so often, on leaving, I wonder if a meal in an elegant room with subdued lighting and quiet conversation can ever be as ripe or delicious as the proverbial chunk of bread and lump of cheese in the fresh air with a river view? Certainly it is not that much more expensive, the river view comes at such a cost these days, every modern city in the world having finally realised the pleasure of water and priced their dirty old riverside or waterfront or sea wall or boardwalk accordingly. In the old days, when rivers were full of filth and traffic and we could not control their tides, the choice for those who could afford it was to look away from the water, to turn the backs of their buildings to it. In time though, roads became our dirty passageways and now the water is the view of choice. It is the place where people stand, gazing out and down, demanding explanation from a flow that has existed long before us and will, global warming notwithstanding, continue on. The river will always continue, no matter what gets in its way. Which is how I come, at the appointed time, in the correct place, with due formality and careful ceremony, to be staring down at the bloated body of my lover.

The Seine was not made for death, there has been the occasional broken princess at its side, but by and large Parisians have done well to keep their bloodied and often headless corpses firmly in the squares, on dry land – not easy when the square is an island – but they've done pretty well. The polite man in a white coat is telling me they pulled her from the river just over a day ago, then brought her here. She had no bag, no wallet, no phone, no identifying tags. She had my name and number, written small, folded smaller, in the discreet gold charm on her discreet gold bracelet. My French is schoolgirl French at the best of times, good for menus and directions and, once, for flirting with young soldiers in New Caledonia, drunken conversations with Spanish relations where French is our only common language – confronted with Marie-Claude's bloated body and seaweed hair, the best I could do was stutter no, *non*, *encore non*, and eventually *qui, c'est elle* – Marie-Claude.

After that came a long time of asking questions, her home, her details, her family. I suggested they call her husband, he'd know these answers. I gave them her home number, a junior was sent to call, returned saying there was no reply. Well, no, he was probably still at work. Why did she carry my number on her? I didn't know. I didn't know she did. Were we good friends? Yes we are. Were. Were we lovers? Yes. We had been. A long time ago. When did I last see her? It has been a month, I was due to visit next week. We both have lives of our own, we did not see each other all that often. Just enough. They said they would probably have more questions for me later, there were certain things they didn't understand. I expect one of them was that the water in her lungs was not the same as the water in the river. I didn't suggest this though, if they hadn't figured it out yet, they would in time. They asked me for my passport and requested I didn't leave the city. I told them I

65

understood. I would be as helpful as I possibly could. I cried. Both in truth and for effect. I was – am – sad for her. They were very grateful for my help. And I think they believed me, it's always hard to be sure of the truth in translation.

More than four hours had passed by the time I left. I assumed they'd have someone follow me, if only to make sure I didn't jump in the river as well. She didn't jump, they must know that. I walked a long time by the water and it was cold and damp, but that felt right. I had expected her to look bad, to look dead. I hadn't thought about her being ugly, dirty, un-suited to the place. Marie-Claude could never have been suited to that place. The light was far too white. Eventually, when I had walked far enough and long enough I found a bar and began to drink. I drank to my good health and her bad death. I drank to a night in Paris when I came here with a girlfriend and left with a drunken Glaswegian squaddie. I drank to the birthday lunch I ate once in a half-broken mausoleum in Père Lachaise, wet and alone and angry. I drank to the day I showed my mother Paris, she who never thought she'd visit the city of light and found it pretty, but wanting. She could not abide tourists, and I did not know what else to show her, not then. I did not know Paris so well then, did not have Marie-Claude's desire to guide me. I drank to him, the husband, how good he had been, how useful, how loving, how lovely. What a good husband and what a good lover. And I drank to her and to me.

Late that night, very late, I have no idea exactly how late, I was not looking at watches or clocks, paying attention to opening hours or closing, I took a taxi to a hotel I remembered from many years ago, a hotel that had nothing to do with her or with me. I leaned against the door and rang the bell until a furious night porter let me in and I bribed him with a fifty euro note to give me a bed for the night. The young woman who had been shadowing me since I left the mortuary waited on the other side of the road until I was shown to a room, drunkenly closed my curtains and, half an hour later, turned off my light. She waited an extra fifteen minutes to be sure, and then trod wearily home. I expect she thought police work might be more fun.

And now I am sober. I am no actress, I admit that, but it is easy to persuade a young woman watching at a distance of twenty feet that grief is drunkenness, lust is love, despair merely an absence of hope.

I arrange my bag, collect my things. I was in this hotel last week, left a case with the friendly night porter. He is a better actor than his work record would show, I thought he really was angry when he answered the door. Or perhaps it was just a way for him to demand the fifty I gave him instead of the twenty we had agreed. Either way, he has done as requested. It is all here. The case with my new clothes and the wig, glasses and keys. The keys to her apartment, our apartment, the home in which I loved Marie-Claude. Our Paris home. I had thought it special and separate, I did not know there were two other keys she also kept as well as the one home she shared with her husband, other apartments she maintained. She was very good at it, the hiding, the lies. Me too. I get changed as quickly as I can, leave the front door looking like a different woman. Even if the watcher has stayed longer than I believe she has, she will not see me now.

~

Those people complaining at the Gare du Nord are right, it is easy to get in and out of the country. It is easy not to have your passport checked on leaving Britain when you journey to Bilbao in a friend of a friend's yacht. When you arrive in a tiny seaside village early in the morning where no-one cares where you've come from, as long as you are prepared to spend money. It is simple to take one train to Barcelona and then another through to Toulouse and buy a car and drive to Paris to meet your lover's furious husband. I don't suppose, however, that entirely white group of protestors at the Gare du Nord were complaining about the travel plans of someone like me. A woman growing older becomes more and more anonymous. A wig with more grey than brunette, makeup carelessly applied, dull clothes that don't quite fit, plain and low heeled shoes – the mask of a middle aged mother is not a difficult disguise and the vanity pangs when passing a mirrored shop front are a price well worth paying for the gift of near-invisibility in the eyes of the young men who man the passport and customs desks.

I hurry away. To a place he has told me of. We meet there in secret, in case he too is being watched. We burn her diaries. I do this as myself, wig and false clothes removed. The light of the small fire keeps me warm, as does his skin. We are careful. It is too good to spoil, this being together. When the work is done, her words burned, he turns to the little case he brought with him, takes out a picnic of bread and cheese and wine, and we toast each other. Our very good fortune to have found each other. And we thank her, for the introduction. In an hour it will be time for me to hurry back to the hotel, hide this other me, he will need to get to the markets, to carry on, as a good widower, and a better restaurateur, in dependable grief.

It began six months ago. He called and asked me to come. So I did. He made the travel arrangements, explained what he had decided needed to happen. We met at the restaurant, late, when only Daoud was still there, hosing down the floor, sluicing away bread and blood and grease so the kitchen would be clean for the morning. Daoud was surprised to see me and, I quickly understood, disappointed. His boss shouted at him for staying so late, taking so long, told him to fuck off, there were plenty of other illegal immigrants hungry for work. I said I did not know that Daoud was illegal, the patron did not either, not for sure, but the way his employee ran from the building suggested he had made the right guess.

We had a drink. One then another. He explained how he found out, the confrontation, the confession. First she told him about us and then, horrible and painful, for me to listen to, and – so he said – for him to explain, about the other lover. And the other. Her one husband and her three lovers. A third drink. There is a peculiar sadness in finding yourself one of many, we are human, we search for the tiny spark of difference. I was the only woman in her selection of lovers, for that I was grateful, a little.

Her latest conquest was a young man, totally besotted, telling all and sundry apparently, not aware of the rules of engagement, the tradition that his attitude ought to have been quiet and careful. The husband was worried for his wife. Worried that other people would realise what she'd been doing, uncover her lies. That they too, would see her for the beautiful whore she was. I said I did not think her a whore, he said we were the ones who paid for her charms. In kind, in love, in our constant waiting for her to return. It was not a financial transaction, but a debt paid was still a debt paid. I began to see his point of view.

I had known about her drug habits, had thought them part of her charm really, a hint of access to a world I had never understood, touching the glamour of oblivion when I touched her. He told me it was worse than that, the new young man fed her habits, enjoyed them with her. He said it was becoming a problem, she only saw me once a month, she was able to make her use look as tidy as I believed it was, but in truth, she was further gone than I realised. Further away than I realised.

He fed me that first night. After all the talking and the tears, took me out to the kitchen and fed me. A mouthful of this, half slice of that. A little more wine, another bite, a sip again, bread, cheese, water, wine, meat, bread, wine, wine, wine, him. Fed me himself. I think now I must have known that would happen. I must have walked into the meeting that night and seen him and known we would fuck. Perhaps I had always known, right back when she first took me to the restaurant and ordered my meal for me and made my choices and fed me his food and paraded me in front of his staff. I was complicit in their married games from the beginning and maybe it was inevitable I would switch sides. Certainly it did not feel as if I made a choice that night. He fed me well, I fucked him well, we were both sick with jealousy and love for her. He was a good lover though, as was she. I am not a French woman, either classic or modern. I do not take an absurdly inflated interest in grooming or diet or accessories – she did, we were her accessories – I am though, inordinately interested in passion. Food and passion. He was skilled in both. Both take careful preparation, he was well planned.

He became my lover, she continued as my lover. She continued with her other lovers. She became increasingly indiscreet as the fervour for her young man increased. As I explained, she did not look like the classic televisual drug addict, the more she played with the young man though, the more he enjoyed her illicit largesse, the wider her mouth, spilling secrets. Eventually her husband decided the time had come. *Aux grands maux les grands remèdes*. Cliché is so French.

I would come to visit her, tell her I knew about her young lover. We would arrange to meet him. There would be a scene, somewhere public. I would force from her confession of their desire. Then I would reveal I also knew of the other lover. Daoud, the washer of filthy dishes in her husband's kitchen. She would deny, fight, shout, and finally, worn down by my heartbreak, agree. Admit. Admit in front of the young man, who would not be sober or clean, who would vow to do something about it. And when her body was found, a day or a week later, the mark of suspicion would be ready on his brow.

It was complicated, uncertain, not at all possible to guarantee what would happen. And yet, in the hotel room bed, in his wide arms, with his food in my belly and his kiss in my mouth, I was persuaded it could all work out. If not exactly as planned, then at least go some of the way towards making the potential true. All we really needed was for her to admit and for him to become angry.

I suppose I could have said no. At any time really, I could have taken my jealousy and fury home with me, traveled away from that city and never seen her again, left them to their desire and bitterness and passion. But I agreed with him, it wasn't fair, she wasn't fair. One understands the role of spouse, or of mistress, either of these make sense. And a spouse knows there is the chance to be cuckolded, a mistress understands she is not first. But a third lover? A fourth? He was right. She was taking the piss. And besides, after just a short while, I quite liked the idea of having him to myself. He was – is – a very attractive man. If not conventionally so. But then I am not, unlike so many Frenchwoman, a lover of convention.

And it appears the plans of her husband, my lover-chef, have worked. I dressed in the disguise he chose for me, traveled as another woman, hid in this city and drowned another woman. Now she is dead and she is not beautiful, the drowned are not beautiful. I have been here a week. First the police came to speak to Daoud, but he had an alibi, he was washing dishes. Plenty of people saw him doing so. The husband had an alibi – he was working, in the kitchen, talking to his customers, creating art from raw ingredients, feeding the discerning masses. The young man did not have an alibi. He was sitting at home that night, alone, shooting up with the heroin substitute she brought him from her office, using the syringe she brought him from her office. Her husband told the police about her lovers, her drug habits, her hidden life. He did not tell the police how we parceled her up in restaurant waste bags and carried her to his van, more often used for transporting sides of beef and mutton, and we took her to the river and we let her fall. So much is hidden under cover of darkness. And London has more CCTV cameras than any other city in Europe. But not Paris, those ugly cameras spoil the view. I told the police about our relationship. They were surprisingly ready to believe a respected medical professional could behave in such a manner, for them, the addition of lust to substance multiplied readily into disaster. It made it simple too, for them to understand the jealousy of her young lover, his head swimming, his hands holding her beneath the water. Crime passionnel is no longer a defence of course, but I trust his time in prison may help him with his addiction problems. *Tout est bien qui finit bien.*

I did not have an alibi. But then I was not in France. My passport proves it, the strong security both our countries now pride themselves on proves it. There may have been a middle aged woman in a grey wig and ill-fitting clothes at some point. She may have been in France, in Paris, but she was not noticed.

I miss her, of course, though not too much, I suspect we were nearing the end of our time anyway, everything has its time. And I have my new lover now, he who feeds me so well. Too well almost. It is lucky my own husband and children demand so much energy at home, keeping me busy, I might get fat otherwise. Family is so important, isn't it?

A SWIMMER'S TALE

I HAVE COME HERE to escape. To forget about the love that never was. (Not true of course, but right now, I would prefer the never was.) I can bear never was far more easily than never will again. Less present pain in return for denying earlier pleasure. I am raw and can no longer imagine what the earlier pleasure might have been. It is all hurt, all loss. And still there is no word, no sign, from you. I am melodrama abandonment, but find no enjoyment in my over-the-top. I've always placed far too much hope in the possibility of eternal clairvoyance for lovers. The possibility of love for lovers.

Girlfriends and boyfriends and ex-lovers and maybe-lovers and concerned mother smiles have all offered helpful advice. The same helpful advice. I was counselled warm beaches, hot sun, hotter bodies. I was counselled sun and sea and surf and alcohol and illicit drugs if at all possible and beyond that, over and above the hedonism of sinning skin, I was counselled hedonism of the flesh. Let them get in. Anyone, any flesh, any man, any woman. Just let someone in, not too deep, but far enough, fill enough of that aching gap and then you won't notice it quite so much. The pain, the loss, the yawning void of the full urn on my mantelpiece. (You'd think after almost a year I'd have done something with it, scattered them somewhere for God's sake. My friends think it's time I did something with it. They're quite possibly right. Their rightness is why I'm here.)

My friends think it's high time I did something with you. But I'm still waiting for a sign, a smile, a cool breeze in the middle of the night from a draft-proofed double-glazed window. You promised you'd let me know it was all right. I'm still waiting. How hard can it be for you to break back through? Is your love really so held by traditional physics? Where's the quantum leap of desire you promised me? I'm looking for miracles and seeing darkness magnified through tears. I'm looking for hope and losing you to black holes.

The obvious correctness of my friends' and family's suggestions though, is why I'm here now, why I'm by the sea. Come to find myself again. (They actually meant come to lose you for the first time, come to let you go, though no-one had the guts to say so.) I think perhaps I was supposed to try Barbadian lust, Bondi bonding, cruise the cruisers and find one for me. (Maybe not the latter, even my most desperate mates don't think seventy-year-old rich Americans are my type.) Instead I have chosen Wales. Anglesey. Peninsula insular. Like me. Like I've become. I used to be the outgoing one of our pairing, the loud one. There seems little point now. Without my other there is nothing for my shadow to fall against. I find I am undefined.

You found me too loud always. In bed, in bath, in Bath. In hotels especially. Too thin walls letting through my too loud desire. You tried to hush me, shut me up. You tried to shut me. Impossible. I blossomed open, time lapse photography fast, when I met you. And stayed that way – it's why daily life scrapes against my open flesh now – I do not know how to close up again. Not since you. You loved to go away, summer killed you in London and you made a motorway maid of me too. We found the finest – and grottiest – hotels in the land, and the so many others. As long as they were within the reach of the sea, or sunshine, or just a running tap if that was all we could manage. You needed water and I needed you. Need you.

At first I thought this was a mistake. There was too much of a sense that you might be round the next corner, hiding in the headway. I kidded myself for a whole half a day that we had arranged for you to meet me later. I do not like to dine alone. It takes no time at all to eat a three course meal by myself and even the best intentioned kitchen staff cannot maintain the pace when there is no knife-and-fork banter to fill up the clock space necessary for perfectly sautéed meat. You did not come to the table. I offered your glass to Elijah, but he wasn't thirsty either. I drank it myself instead. I have drunk alone far too many of the bottles I used to share with you. It's one way to get to sleep. It's the only way to get to sleep. Which is still infinitely preferable to waking up.

Milos. Cycladian sea island. Circadian rhythms shot to fuck by the fuck shooting through me to you and back again. We are on a tourist boat charting the island circumference. You marvel at my bravery as I dive into cliché-clear waters. I marvel at your bravery as you dive into me. I swim beneath the sea and look up to you, magnified by the depths of sea-through ocean. You are an amplified version and the water might be sea, might be me. My love/lust/lost-in-you tears make you huge. You fill the space of my vision. You fill the space of me.

The first night here it rained seven hours solid. Howling rain pelted by a broken wind against my window. I knew how it felt. I lay awake as I do so often now, waiting for you. Wondering if here you might be able to find me again. I worry that you are lost out there, elemental soul beating against closed doors unable to worm-hole your way through to me. And then too, I worry that there's nothing to worry about. That there is none of you left. That the reason you have not managed the Cathy/Heathcliff reunion we promised each other is because there is nothing to reunite. I am real, corporeal. You are not. I should hope that your present nothingness is the truth, hope for your sake that you aren't wandering the darkness trying to find me. Should, don't. My grief is still selfish enough to deny you a peaceful nothing. I just want to touch you again. (And even when I say that, I know it's not true. One touch would never be enough. I would keep you with me forever.) Your departure has made a genie-keeper of me. I'd lock you back in that urn quick as kiss you. I'd lock you back in my flesh quick as love you. Love you quick again.

Sydney sunshine. You and I and the antipodean sky, lost in the sharp blue, astounded by the fierceness of the sun, astonished that while it burnt my skin, you burnt my lips more, branded ourselves with each other. My body was made to hold yours. There were wonders to see and you ignored them to look at me. We were not good tourists, I could send home no postcards of the fine sights they offered us, I had no 'wish you were here' when I was with you. Your topography was more than enough.

There is a man here, also alone. I think the breakfast waitress would like us to talk to each other. I think she is more interested in the morning ease of having to clear just the one table, than the possibility that this man and I might find conversation possible. We don't talk, but I do begin to watch him.

He eats toast and marmalade, no butter, as you did. But his toast is cut into quarters, eaten carefully, he does not crush a slice in half as you did and finish one piece in three mouthfuls. He seems to have more time than you did. I'd steal it from him if I could, give you his time. Your death has made a murderer of me. The man is slow and deliberate. Every morning he sets out, walks the mud flats of the shallow tide. He has binoculars and telescope. It is a wet summer, he watches shore birds, writes them down in a notebook. At least that's what I imagine he's doing – sighting, writing. As if simply seeing is enough. He does not need to touch as well. It's a skill I would do well to learn.

Hot Paris summer. All the Parisians have left, abandoning their over-heated city to we foolish tourists. You and I are over-heated and weighed down with shopping and crowded by jostling Italian school children. We fight on the Metro, an argument about nothing, escalating to everything. It is not unusual for us to fight and even so, every time we do, I think it means the end. Still I cannot stop myself. Run up the stairs and into the sweltering city and far from you. Will not back down, don't remember where this began, probably don't care, and yet am so caught up in the emotion, the wave of your fury and my anger, that I have no way of coming back to you. You come back to me instead, remind me that however much I hate you, you are going nowhere without me. That I can push you away as much as I want, beat you off with my violent words, but you're not leaving. I glare at you and refuse to admit my relief, my gratitude at your astonishing staying-power. It's impressive. And I do believe you. Believe I cannot push you away. That night we lay in a hot bed, desultory ceiling fan

*stirring humid air around our dark-painted room, sticky skin
making the slow approach, remembering who we are because
we are with each other. And I did believe you when you said I
couldn't send you away. You were right of course, it wasn't me
who sent you. It was summer.*

On the third morning the sun was shining when I awoke. I
was surprised by the brighter light through the heavy curtains.
Did not understand the faint ease of spirit, tried to banish the
half-smile playing with my features, but it wouldn't leave my
face. It was late when I woke, two solo wine bottles conspiring
in my hot, heavy slumber. I'd missed breakfast, missed the man
with his carefully quartered toast. I dressed without showering
first – you'd have been appalled – pulled on yesterday's tired
clothes, dragged my matted hair back into a careless pony tail.
There was a new urgency, I didn't know why or what for, I did
know I'd better get out there and use it before my inebriate
brain woke up properly and grief lethargy hit again. The sun
was hot on my covered arms, your old jumper that I've been
wearing half the time for most of a year was not meant for
summer, not even British summer. I pulled the sleeves up to
my elbows and looked at my pale arms, thin since you. Bony
fingers reaching out for a hand to hold. I stopped on the road
above the shore and saw the man, his telescope trained on a
rock far out, exposed by the low tide, I saw wheeling dots
around the rock, no doubt he saw and knew his prey, jotted
notes on salt-damp paper, categorized, called and caught. He
watched the birds for an hour or so, I watched him for almost
as long. It was peaceful and warm, not enough tourists had
lasted the wet week for the remaining few to disturb me over
much. Those who had stayed were families with too many

small children and too few large bank balances to move on to the next place the sun might be. The shore was blessedly free of hand-holding couples who might have rubbed sea-salt in my fresh wounds. It is close to a year, I know, but the wounds are as fresh as the day you made them, ripping yourself away from my grasp. They stay fresh, I like them that way. I understand them that way. The man began to pack up his equipment and I quickly moved on, up the hill, beyond the headland where the wind is fresher and cooler. I did not want him to see me watching. He might equate distraction with interest, and I can no longer manage polite conversation. Strangers are not usually equipped to deal with unexpected tears. I did not use to cope so well either. Now the salt-flow is my norm. You always preferred sea water to fresh. How nice to know I am still pleasing you. (I would rather not please you.)

Venice. They all said not to go in summer. They were right. Would have been right if we had been tourists, clammy bodies cramming St Mark's Square, over-flowing flesh flooding into the Lido overflow. But we were not tourists you and I. I had not travelled to the lagoon to marvel at Tintoretto or applaud the bravery of the Guggenheim collection. Instead I took a hotel room-bound long weekend to marvel at the delicate flesh tones of you, to applaud the priceless modern collection, astonishing bravery of spirit, the audacity and shock that was only you. Your body offered to me on cool white sheets, your self laid out with room service care, the touch and taste of you making a bland white bread of their coffee, biscotti, bruchetta, prosecco, proscutio, prandial-offered prospect. Childhood-myth and long awaited Venice lay before me, open plate, offered wide. I closed the shutters on the grounded visitors of

the grand vista, Grand Canal, you were all the view I needed. I
toured you that weekend. Unlikely rest weekend away, I went
home exhausted and thin. Who could ask for more?

Since then I have been offered another chance to view you,
laid out on equally cool white sheets. They said it might have
helped. But I wasn't interested in making it better. They could
not make you better, you were my very best, so why bother?
I closed the wide eye-shutters on their kind offer. Some sights
should remain unseen wonders; wonder-full, awe-full. Awful.

You and I swimming. You have always swum further,
faster, deeper than me. I would struggle to keep up, against the
current, against the waves, against my grain. I am really a land
person, understand dirt, rocks, hills, mountains, prefer my
horizon bordered with recognizable jigsaw edge pieces. You
like a long straight line of water against the sky, would swim
far out until I was left behind, bobbing in the shallows, strain-
ing salt-splashed eyes for your return. No change there then.
But I always enjoyed the intensity of your enjoyment, happily
lay hours on the beach, leathering my skin as you watered
your parched soul, several summers of block-buster reading
discarded for the better-seller option of reviewing you.

Fifth morning and I found myself watching the man again.
This time from my bedroom window, wet day, no sleep, no
energy to make the dressed politeness of dining room breakfast, I sipped already cold tea with UHT milk and couldn't
taste the difference anyway. He walked through the morning
drizzle, apparently untouched by the disgruntled irritation
of bed and breakfasters all along the coast, their one-week-
a-year panic settling and sending out just-suppressed fury, a
heavy wave of pissed-off mist lining the damp shore. It seemed

though that perhaps this was just what the man wanted. Empty coastline, morning haze, ugly mudflats of low tide exposing the bird breakfast smorgasbord. Like him, you wouldn't have cared about the weather, might even have welcomed the rain, clearing the sea for your endeavours alone. But you wouldn't have seen his sights. Your eye would have been trained on the fuzzy horizon, the thin grey line blurred by the cool land and the warm rain. You would have walked right past him, run even, to get into the water, drench your skin in its welcoming cold. But I watched him searching carefully, patiently training his eye on something too far to touch, too wild to get close, yet there. Within his sights. Watching and noting and writing down the real. And then I found I'd been watching the man for three hours. He'd been watching the birds for three hours. It was almost midday, the clouds began to clear and the beach-bound families re-found their summer resolve – we will play on the beaches, come rain or shine. The shine finally came and so did they, deserting the indoor shopping malls for the outdoor version. The bird man turned away. Clearly needed fewer people for his telescopic foray. It seemed that perhaps no people might suit him better. Made sense to me. And I began to think about what he was looking at, that he seemed to have made it his job to view what was actually there.

When they told me what had happened, it was impossible to believe. Not that I chose not to believe, or couldn't understand, simply too far-fetched for truth. We'd talked about it. Late-night lover conversations, 'How will I survive without you?', 'You won't ever have to.' 'I'm never leaving you.' 'I'm never leaving you.' 'If anything ever happens to me I'll come back.' 'Promise?' 'Promise.' But it wasn't something else that happened to you. Not something outside, beyond our control, no freak accident, creeping disease that took you. They told me that you took yourself, the creeping dis-ease of accidental freak. You should have come to find me, confided in me. You should have cooled yourself swimming in me, but while I could always lose myself in you, soothe myself in you, it seems the reverse was not true. In summer, in London, sweltering city of land-locked people and grid-locked cars, you could find no water-marked horizon to cool yourself, so you swam out into the sky instead. Diving towards a sharp line horizon that could not be real, swimming yourself to the same place.

And it seems I've been doing the same. Training my telescopic eye on the not-there. Scanning impossible horizons for a blessed untruth, notebook and pen poised to record the self-created hope.

The next day, a solid night's sleep for the first time in nearly a year, and again I am up before the sun has made it through the thick morning drizzle. My bags are packed, my room tidied, and I'm on the shore before all the other visitors who have learned to wait until at least five hours of daylight has burnt away the rain. I carry you to the shore as you sometimes tried to carry me. Picking me up and stumbling a few feet to dump me in the water, both of us tumbling in the waves and each other. I carry the full urn and take this chance to look at you, really see what is here, not my dream of you. The truth is that you are ashes. That is all you are. And ashes cannot come back to me. I can see the bird man, maybe three hundred feet away, his telescope trained on the high cliff to our right. The breakfast waitress told me he had hoped to sight a pair of gannets this week, that someone had told him they had been seen around here recently staying on too long into summer, a special treat for the watcher. She told me gannets mate for life. It's a nice idea, but I don't know much about birds, don't care much about birds. It turns out the hope of flight was your thing, not mine. The man raises a hand to wave to me, after all, we've seen each other every morning, every day, for almost a week now. But I don't respond. I have a job to do. Something real of my own to view. I have the truth of you to concentrate on. The water is warmer than I had expected. I walk out to almost waist deep. There is very light rain, a thin horizon of pale grey, the certainty of bright sunshine in another hour or so. I'm training my vision only on what is here, now. I'm holding the urn that is holding you and walking out to do the right thing.

Mid-summer, warm water, me flesh, you ashes. Mid-summer, warm water, me here, you gone. Mid-water, hot summer, you're gone, I'm here. Mid-me, then mid-you, scatter the summer of you in the warm water around me. Swimming with summer you in the warm water, scattering around the swimming me. Me swimming in you, in letting go, leaving you, swimming around, scattering in me. You and me and summer water, the warmth of the waves and a thin grey horizon that is growing stronger with the hotter sun, bluer as the bright light burns off the misty grey. I am letting you go. Like the bird man, I will concentrate only on what I can see. Breathe in deep only what I can see. Breathe in. I can see you. Sea me. We too are warm. We two are warm.

Later, the bird man, unfortunately not much of a swimmer himself, said it had certainly looked as if the woman knew where she was swimming to.

BEING THE BARONESS

I HAVE BECOME THE Baroness. I almost don't know how it happened, as if the time that passed did so on grandma's footsteps, creeping up to catch me out. One day I was Liesl, wet dress of palest pink clinging to my sixteen-going-on-twenty-one breasts, panting the possibilities of all things male beyond my ken (sure they were, Barbie) and the next, I am the Baroness. Madam not Mademoiselle, Senora not Senorita. I am the adult woman, I pour the tea, I drink pure and simple cocktails that do not have double entendre names, I have a winter wardrobe that goes into storage with the first cuckoo. I did not mean to get here. Be her. I didn't know it could happen so soon. Twenty-six years so soon.

I'm very well groomed, I do not mourn the flesh of my youth. I have no cause for complaint against myself, the outer layer, the visuals remain beyond reproach. The gold sheath dress I wore for my last dinner would not stretch to fit half the younger women I know. They don't seem to try very hard any more, these young girls, they think it's easy, that it's just coming to them, that they deserve it all. Our sacrifices, my sacrifice, handed over on a plate of what you will. The young women I see in the streets, on the screens, in their flabbiness of youth – late twenties, early thirties even some of them, still certain there's time to take it in hand, fix themselves up, make the flesh work for them before the moment has passed. When it already has. (If you know there is a moment to pass – then believe me, my dear, it's passed you by.) They are late already, these younger women of my acquaintance, distant relation. Some of them too late now, some of them were always too late, born too late, made too late by their own ignorance or intentional unknowing. I see these girls-to-women and understand that they have missed the moment of conquest without realising, observe the ones who will never look back on a time of iridescent beauty, golden power. I can. I do. Perhaps that is what makes it so hard now. How much I know of then.

There are seven stages of woman.

First is Gretl, small and stocky, body too sturdy for the delicacy of childhood. A Gretl is cute and keen to grow, and she is interchangeable with Marta, the forgotten girl, the other one. (Dark hair, just a year older, no-one remembers her name.) Next comes Brigitta. Ten years old and for Brigitta the world is all books and possibility and hiding in the pages from an outside that threatens too soon to intrude, the beginnings of womanhood that are alien, frightening. Brigitte wanders lost in the space made by the woman she is yet to become. Louisa and Liesl are third and fourth. The interchange between nearly and not quite there. The natural blonde of the classic virgin and the rouged brunette of growing knowing. They represent those few years where the pendulum swings in a single day, a momentous hour, from girl to woman and back again. Ballet to boys, mischief to men.

When I was Liesl I knew nothing. Not really. Certainly I knew bachelor dandies, drinkers of brandies – what young woman does not? (Only the young woman whose words are written by an older man.) I was born knowing the ways of men. What I did not know were the ways of women. And to know only half the truth, is to know close to nothing at all. Men have always been easy for me, moveable, pliable, play-able. Women were my mystery. Myself included. It took time to understand female, she-male, woman. Femininity on the other hand, that was simple. Femininity required merely a giggle of champagne and a dress of swirled organdy. What I learned, what I have acid-etched on my heart, took graduating from girl to woman. And not even aware I had studied. But I keep the knowledge. It is wiser to remember.

I learned that looking good is not good enough. Cunning is also required, and skill to catch him, art to hold him. Yet cunning is not sufficient either, there must also be love. And we had it, my Captain and me. (Lover Captain, not father Captain – I'm telling you an analogy, not a truth.) We had so much love, between us, I certainly had enough for two. And he had enough for me. Until he didn't. Until he had her and she used it, used him, used his love, in that way little girls do, half-women do, using it all up and asking for more, demanding more. I have never asked for more, I am disciplined and self-denying and constrained. My will is the corset that holds me in, tempers my yearning, fits me for the pattern of my life. I have always hated the idea of looking needy, seeming greedy. (Silly me. It was her need he loved the most.)

This is how it was.

When I met Marcus I was just sixteen. He was twenty-eight. Far too young for me they said. Someone to flirt with perhaps, go out with once or twice, learn what I could, but not want, not really want. I would know better when I grew up, look back on this as a romance, a lesson in love. But I knew better even then. Knew that I would grow, and learn and change – and that probably, Marcus would not. He would, as every man does, pick his decade and stay there until his demise. Even then, at sixteen, I knew stasis was his outer form, and change my inner process. That I would change until I became what he required, and then I would do all in my power to stay there for him, and if I could not stay there wholly, I would at least manufacture the perfect mask that made it look as if I had. I had a plan, I expected it to work. And, like most plans, it did for a while. I waited and I matured and I became a lady, woman created of the open articulation of his wants. Marcus never had any qualms about expressing his wants. I developed personal poise and special talents, procured a double degree, an honours education, matriculated myself into Marcus' mistress. At work I had a thriving business career, at home a fantastic act on my back. Front. Knees. All these things in which I have confidence. And nowhere to ply my trade.

Marcus meanwhile had acquired a wife. Of course he had. Who expected him to wait? Every man needs a first wife, someone to ready him for the second. A second wife can wear what she wants, classic gold, dark silver, maybe even tempt the jealous gods in a twist of green and blue. A first wife must always wear white. White suits no woman's complexion, and ankle hiding is for Victorian tables. Every woman looks better in colour, best in black. We are washed out in witless white or worse, the latter day ironic ivory. (How these girls do that without wincing I don't know, they might as well wear the stained sheet to the altar.) I had no intention of being just any other bride, covering my curves and bleaching out my beauty in a simplistic recreation of every other wedding. So I held out, made myself a better mistress as the first wife worsened. Readied myself to come first in second place.

Yes, I could have tried to be the first and only, done my best to take him on and found a way to make him stay. But even then, I knew myself, knew who I would become as well as I knew who he was, and would always be. Marcus needed a woman who was first-wife-material. And I am no-one's material. I am tissue and flesh and blood, cannot be taken in or let out or cut and re-shaped, but by my own design. I just needed him to be ready, for me. And in time, he was. The first wife swept away, the bedroom door unlocked for me. He had always had the key to mine, now I had the key to his as well.

And it was good with Marcus. Passionate and fierce, of course, but also friendly. We were friends. I could make him laugh as no other woman could, read out a stupid newspaper item, recount a chance meeting at my work, act out the conversation I had intentionally overheard in a restaurant three nights earlier. Keeping tidbits for Marcus to enjoy later when we were alone. I knew what pleased him, and he knew my pleasures too. We dined together, drank together, shopped together. Marcus is the only man I have ever let shop for me. He is the only man I ever trusted to get it right. He would leave me naked in the hotel bed and return an hour or so later with something lovely in a box. A necklace, a bracelet, a dress. Something lovely wrapped in pale tissue, carefully boxed by sales assistant hands whose wages could never afford the gift I received so readily.

And when Marcus and I made love every time was like the first time. What more can be said? (Except that every time might also be the last time, I knew that too. Though I'm not sure he did.)

And time passes.

Yes, very well, though I would rather skip right over and move swiftly on, there is the fifth stage. Maria. Number Five. The Julie years. What is there to say of those women who give themselves to this time and stay there forever? That they are complicit, compliant? That their only desire is the ring on the finger, the key to the door, that they will subjugate and subdue their vital selves for the lightest weight of red gold? That they would trade the convent cloister for the marriage bed, maintaining vows of obedience in both, seeing no difference between bride of Christ or Christopher? Of course I despise these women, I was never able to be them – we all despise what we cannot bear to attempt. I could see the advantages, of course I could. Men adore a Maria, just enough verve to stand up to them, just enough sense to lie down in time. In truth, and not a little regret, I simply couldn't shut myself up long enough to say, 'I do, I will' – and sound like I meant it.

Marcus was forty-two, I was thirty – I was just thirty. Young enough to turn heads purely with my youth, old enough to hold them turned with desire. I was wonderful – I am still wonderful, I know that – but I was truly wonderful then. And yet, that damned fifth stage has its charms too. Particularly if the woman knows how to work those charms. And work them she did. Worked them in seeming innocence and clumsy care, worked and wormed her way, right past me, to Marcus. And I attended his second wedding as his only mistress. Only as his mistress.

So we come to the sixth stage of woman, she who is

beautiful and charmed and wealthy and elegant. Who has made herself so, piece by self-created piece. A Baroness who lives her own life on her own terms. And if, one night, stuck in her car with her best friend, she realizes in the pouring rain that she is forty and single, that she is Bette Davis as Margot Channing and all her career is not worth losing her man, if she sinks so low as to think this could be true – then a real Baroness would never dream of saying so out loud. The Baroness is a European invention, she does not indulge in American psychobabble. She swallows down her disappointment, knowing it will keep her thinner than gin, and holds it to herself. The Baroness is all gold. She does not reflect inwards.

I keep it all in, tighter than the leanest muscles my trainer punishes me for daily. And he stayed with me, Marcus, married one wife, then two, and stayed with me. Until he didn't. Until there was a third wife and a third family and he became, not the lover with whom I was friends, but my friend. Marcus began to introduce me as his friend. The first time it happened was a tiny dagger to the bone, the second a tearing rip of sinew, muscle, and flesh, the third by-passed my heart entirely and shot straight through to the spleen, I bit back the bile. I knew then it was the end. And when he introduced me to a sharp young thing in a little black dress that was all angles and curves and perfectly proportioned and sex and restraint and right, not a hint of pink or baby blue in sight, I shook hands with an all-knowing replica of my twenty-years-younger self. I knew I was meeting the second mistress. She was good, I applauded his taste and I hated her, kissed him goodbye and I left the room.

Marcus made his right choices, I made mine. There

was no recrimination, and tears are inappropriate in a silk blouse.

In the end comes the seventh stage – nun. None. I'll have none of that. That choice entails a long black dress, and too high windows. Or widow perhaps, but again the black dress is long and the arms are covered, the legs enslaved to mourning. And a Baroness would never opt for mourning. The Baroness' legs are far too good to hide, their shape demands the rustle of silk stockings, the shush of satin shifting just above the knee. The Baroness' cheekbones are too sharp to be hidden by a wimple or mourning veil.

So I choose again, and always, the little black dress. I slip from the possibility of age and infirmity, of time's revenge, into the calm eternity of ending beautifully. In my own time, on my own terms, in the softest, smoothest black satin dress with gold silk lining. Little dress, narrow body, resolved heart. It is what I intend to do, when the time comes, and it will come soon. All my own choices, just as my whole life has been, since the day I grew up. Since the first day I met him, saw Marcus walking down the path, and looking into his face, I knew exactly how to be what he wanted. Even as I also knew I would never stoop to do it, invert my I to we. My choice is bittersweet, I know that. (What choice is not?) But it is my choice and because of that, it is worth my choosing.

I do not make my plans to leave because Marcus no longer wants me as his lover. I make my plans to leave because I am no longer the woman I was. Age brings me to a time of need, inevitably. And the Baroness is nothing if not self-sufficient.

Afterwards, the ebony coffin too is a little black dress. A satin lining of gold holds me soft and quiet and I am where I always want to be. In the centre, venerated, adored, and doing it all as I want. For myself. In the end, who else is there to do it for? Because the end will come, and each of us will lie alone in our little black dresses, in our little black boxes, in the deep black earth. Quiet, and single. And all the gold rings in the world can't save us from that.

A PARTRIDGE IN
A PEAR TREE

WHEN THE KING of Spain's daughter came to visit me she wore a gown of ivory brocade cut into with diamond lace. On her feet were calfskin shoes and she carried a fan carved from a single elephant tusk. The King of Spain's daughter travelled from Seville to Cordoba by foot, then by carriage to Madrid. She waited two hours at the airport there, bought a Steven King novel and caught an adjoining flight to Barcelona. Unfortunately she left the book – just three chapters in and already dog-eared – in the seat-back pocket on the plane. After a brief diversionary weekend in Sitges, lunch in Tarragona, supper in Girona, she travelled the coast road up to Perpignan. I did not know she was coming, but on the day she left, a week after the feast of the Assumption, I knew something was on its way. I felt it in the water, washed my hands in a porcelain bowl and the cool liquid was heavy with waiting.

I will come to you in the evening, orange blossom in my hair. I will take your hand and hold it to my breast, you will count the beats of my heart. We will never go astray. Daylight may be marred by fog or rain, the moon waxes and wanes, the earth spins on an elliptical axis so that even the rising sun appears to arrive from an altered direction, adjusting the angle of shine from summer to winter. But the Pole Star and the Southern Cross have marked us out. I'm coming. I'll need a cup of tea when I get there. And a good book.

I don't know how she found me. I know why she found me. The tree drew her, of course. Pear tree, not nut tree, no matter what they called it. I should know, I planted the seed. It drew them all, my little tree. Cousins and kings, councillors, counts, and the others too. Those that would steal it, take the harvest, smelt it down, make their own precious things. There are always people waiting to steal what they can, especially from something as generous as my little tree – those welcoming wide open branches. But these were my precious things, they would not be taken. Having planted the seed in the first place – one part organic compost to two parts peat and sand mix – I too was surprised when the tree began. I remember my fifth form biology, I eat bean sprouts, I know what to watch for.

I know what to watch for. The lie of the land, sleight of hand, wedding band. Your ring finger is empty. I will fill it for you.

I watched the seed unfurl and grow. And keep growing. First the kitchen windowsill, then a gentle tempering to the outdoors, terracotta pot bubble-wrapped tight for chilly evenings, by spring the root and branches were strong enough for the ground. London clay, thick and cloying, seemed worth a try. The blossom arrived first. It was not as I had expected, almost too delicate. We had a warm spring this year, lucky spring, a late and easy Easter, four full moons packed into the first three months. I know about trees, fruit and nut. Have read up on them, our local library sees a lot of allotmenteers, books pock-marked by dirty fingers. Usually there must be two trees, male and female, for the promiscuous dancing bees. I had just the one. It wasn't meant to fruit so soon. But it did. How it did. Nutmeg and pear. Pear tree with a little added spice.

I agree with you. After all, if the tree blooms a pear, then surely the branch on which it sits is a pear tree? And pear wood is mine, always has been. Sacred to Athena, Hera, Vishnu-Narayana. (I looked it up online.) I am coming for it. For the gardener too and your rough dirt-working hands. I don't mind a hard journey. I do not believe it is better to travel than to arrive, at least not in second class accommodation. But the approach is valuable, a time of preparation, consideration. I gather myself, the advent of arrival.

Unfortunately one of my neighbours, nosy woman, always chatting over the fence, became interested in the tree's progress. It is the curse of our London terraces – you think I live here because I actually enjoy a recreation of the fifties myth, street-party stories? I certainly do not. Sadly I do not have the wealth to garner anonymity and my interfering neighbour saw the shining leaves. I had tried to shield the heavy flowers from her spying eyes, the prying spies I knew she would tell, a full mouth of secrets dripping from the corner of her curling lips. I built a shed around the tree, open to summer light, closed against winter dark. Glass roofed, glass bricked, creosote-edged beams erected merely for the scent, my shed was a place of translucent light and slow growing ease. I am no DIY expert, B&Q is close to the seventh ring of hell for me, IKEA a Swedish prison. But I tried hard, worked harder and, in the end, I was pretty damn pleased with the result. There are people who enjoy the process of creation. Not me, my moment of satisfaction comes from having it all done and dusted. Ready. Waiting.

I dressed well for the journey, packed better for my arrival. We had some troubles on the way, problems both with transport and accommodation. You have to pre-book Travel Inns far in advance these days and I prefer not to give out my credit card details on the telephone if at all possible, I do not easily believe in strangers. Well, but not easily. Still, we managed. I wore the silk brocade, dark green. It creases least of all my gowns. The diamond cuts can be perilous though, the edges are carbon-dated and sharp. As long as I take care to move with precision my skin generally stays whole. And the calf-skin slippers are very soft, easy to walk in. I have read the new suggestion that even short journeys can cause deep-vein thrombosis, it is best to take precautions. I dance in my slippers whenever possible. Airline stewards usually appreciate the gesture.

Summer took its time and the blossom turned to fruit, growing full and fatter by the day, weighing down the fine branches. There was so much interest I gave in eventually, took the neighbour's interference as an opportunity instead. I offered tickets at my front door, a glimpse of the silver and gold for a tenner. For many of them that was enough. I could still feel her in my waters, it was growing heavier by the day. I worried for the meter, thick sticky ticking through the massy wet. The bill from our beloved Thames Water would no doubt be excessive, and I'd stopped going to work to guard the tree. The universe was perilously close to giving up providing. My quarterly council tax was due as well, gate sales were good, but possibly not quite enough for Lambeth's exorbitance. But still I sat, in the cut-glass shed. I knew something was coming, someone. I trusted her to make it all better. And I trusted my tree. It would not give its treasures up to just anyone, nor offer the fruit to any hand.

I wear a ring on my left hand. Daughter of Athena, the owl that watches from my ring finger itches in a straight line to my heart. Summer grows hotter and the central plains are arid. We travel on, further north. I trust you are worth my journey. (All journeys travel on trust.)

Late summer turned to autumn slipped into the harvest festival, full moon and she on her way.

I can smell you. Your spice scent dragged me up through France, the TGV faster still for my nose's demands. Silver nutmeg in a hot toddy, silver nutmeg mixed into smooth mashed potato, silver nutmeg grated on rice pudding. You will remove the ugly milk skin before I see it, I know you will. The comfort dishes of my desire have dragged me drugged with aroma through the Channel Tunnel. Just twenty minutes and a cheering group of school children to cross under water into the sceptred isle, I dance the aisle and smile on England. Aquitaine's Eleanor would have loved this. Though perhaps she was more of a cinnamon girl.

There is a pear too you know. Juicy pear, ripe pear. An always-ripe pear. Never too hard, never too soft, just right little Goldilocks, this pear is always just right. It will not rot nor drop from the tree. Well, you wouldn't expect any less from a golden one, would you? Not gilded you understand, but actually, truly, properly gold. So why all the fuss about the silver nutmeg? There is also a glistening gleaming golden pear. That's a big deal too isn't it? I tell you Marco Polo, the spice route has a lot to answer for.

Slowing down now for the Kent countryside, hops picked, apples stored in cool barns. And then houses become clustered, back gardens open their faces to morning-tired commuters, the train steadies me forward to Waterloo winter and tube tickets and escalator and lift and change to overground train and then street and 45 bus and you. Your house. Your garden shed of glass. So this is it. I am come. I ring the bell.

The doorbell is ringing. I can hear it. My little tree can hear it too, the sap rises. Nutmeg and pear sing softly to themselves, ringing through their metal. She has arrived, our very own personal pronoun of what happens next. I was eager before, nervous but eager, now I am just scared. What if I don't like her? What if she doesn't like me? What if I don't matter and all the fuss is, yet again, only for the tree? The doorbell is ringing. I rise from my ripped yellow stool – its plastic coating once matched a fine fifties formica table – and open the shed door. It has been raining. I've been in here since late light last night and now there are spider webs in my way. Picked out in individual wet droplets, crossing my path. The strung webs are pretty, in a modernist Christmas decoration, silver-and-plain-crystal-nothing-too-gaudy, kind of way. They are also a sticky nuisance as I walk back into the house, through the kitchen, down the hall to the front door, leaving a dozen homeless spiders behind me as I go. I'll say this for the King of Spain's daughter, she certainly knows how to ring a bell.

The door opens away from me and you are just as I expected. Tall and lean and the tanned skin of your face is fine-etched from the many hours of gardening and building work during the long summer. You are beautiful, but then I would not have expected less. The seed would not have pushed through the dirt unless it wanted to take a good look at you. I stand on your doorstep, looking over your shoulder into the hall. Your house is a little more suburban than I would have thought. That dado rail will have to go. And I'm not sure about the coir matting covering the stripped and sanded floorboards. I know they are appropriate for the area, your age and your social group, but isn't it rough on bare feet first thing in the morning? We shall see.

She was short. I knew she was short because I had to lower my eye level when I opened the door. For some reason I had expected a taller woman. Dark, with long hair and longer limbs. The flamenco dancer classic I guess. Not that she wasn't beautiful. And the orange blossom was a good touch. She did have the long dark hair, dark skin, big round brown eyes – a young Susan Dey, after the braces and the faked piano playing, and many years before LA Law turned her blonde. I was a bit rubbish there, at the door, just staring. It's not every day I greet royalty on my doorstep. The Queen doesn't come south of the river all that often, can't get the cabs I expect. I wasn't sure how to address her. Your highness. Your holiness. Darling.

You stand aside and I enter. I am used to a little more ceremony in welcome, but you will learn in time. I will teach you. I am a good teacher, have schooled both willing and unwilling pupils. Between us there is a shy glance, sly glance, and I note your dilating pupils. Mine too I expect. We have both felt the strong desire stretching from here to my home, reaching halfway across this continent. As I journeyed closer our joint passion compacted, a black hole into which all wanting poured. My suitcases are piled beside your wheelie bin, you pay the porters from my Lulu Guinness purse, take the bags in your hands and then begin a stumble of uncertainty. Upstairs or downstairs, where is my lady's chamber? You are reticent and do not know which room to show me first. I lead the way, unerring sense of direction, up the stairs, first right and into the bathroom. No bidet, how English. I wash my travel-dirtied hands. Your water is heavy, isn't it? Is that what they mean by the limescale problem here? We will install filters. Next week. For now I take your builder's hands, gardener's hands, hold them in mine which are clean and a little wet still. There is a hardened blister just north of your lifeline. I will smooth that, soothe that, my tongue reaches for the scrape of rough skin. You are coy, slow, I hear an intake of breath and smile. There is time. How about a cup of tea?

She unpacked, I put the kettle on. I was just starting to worry that perhaps she'd want some girlie herbal tea and all I had were builders' bags, when she walked into the kitchen carrying a small wooden chest. She had changed, jeans and a t-shirt. But she still wore the calf-skin slippers. Fair enough, that diamond lace looked dangerous. Lovely, but dangerous. She sat the chest on the kitchen table and showed it to me. It was well made, old. There were nine drawers, each one lined in silver with a different faintly scented selection of fine leaves. She took the pot from me – our fingers crossed again – and began to mix her brew. Half a teaspoon of this, a quarter of that, one full of another. Each one dropped into the pot, falling with a gentle shush. Then the boiling water and then the wait. Five minutes she said. Long enough to take a good long look. I thought she meant the tree, opened the back door, pointed the way past the ripped and hanging webs. She did not follow. It was not yet time. She meant me, I was to be looked at. Inspected is not too fine a definition for the looking that began again with my hands, lingered on my forearms, dwelt on my shoulders and back and neck and then came to my face.

I want to see you. See what they do not see when they sweep past you and out to the little tree. I want to see the one who planted the seed.

She touched my eyelids and the delicate veined skin yearned to open for her. She ran the back of a smooth-buffed thumbnail across my eyelashes and each one blinked for her, severally and individually. She traced the print of her index finger along my eyebrows and down to the tired shadows of my long waiting – I knew for the first time the perfect circularity of my eye sockets. She lingered with the quiet wrinkles at the time–folded corners, laughter lines, worry lines, crying lines. I could have told her the content of each one. She did not ask. And then, finally, she licked the ball of her left little finger and brought her own liquid to my dry tear duct. It was a surprise and a relief. The tea was ready. We had a cup each. And chocolate bourbons. They were new to her. She ate five and a half.

When I kiss you the taste on your tongue is of these English biscuits. They are nice, plain. Later I will feed you on my food. When I lick your hand the flavour is of your garden, London clay and spider's webs, clean and dirty at the same time. When you hold me I am nearly naked. For a woman used to boned corsets, wide dresses, heavy gowns, this t-shirt is flimsy and easily removed. (Remove it easily.) When we lie together on your kitchen floor I wonder in passing about the cleanliness, how recently this room was swept do you have a cleaner will you clean for me wash for me touch for me love for me. I wonder in passing and then you are passing over my body around my skin under my heart and I into you and you back to me and this is why I have come, why I am here, where I will come back to. You are easy, quiet, slow, ready. The wait was worth it, I hear the song of bending boughs from the shed at the bottom of your garden.

I'd never had sex with royalty before either. Fortunately the protocols weren't all that different. She was smooth and soft except just at the waistband where the diamond lace had cut into her, leaving a lattice of small scratches, light scabs for gently easing free. When we were done with the kissing and the turning and the laying and the wanting we went upstairs together to wash. I ran her a bath and she lay back into the water. It was heavy and held her close. I would have climbed in with her, but she said that would not be right. Not on a first date. I showered when she was finished, cleaned the tub and wiped it down. I pulled her long black hairs from the plug hole, dried, combed and plaited them. Put away the thin rope of hair in a heart-shaped music box left behind by my last lover.

You are storing me, shoring me up, just in case. There is no need. I'm staying now.

She said she was hungry again, that travelling always gave her an appetite and the airline food appeared to have become even worse since the imposition of further security checks.

I don't mind the security, really I don't, I appreciate both the necessity and the effort involved, but I am very disturbed by that whole plastic cutlery thing.

She said she needed flesh, meat, wanted to suck small

bones. I offered a frozen chicken from the freezer, fish fingers maybe, but she had come prepared. Pulled enamel pots and aluminium pans from the Luis Vuitton, condiments and utensils from her handbag, and an A-Z from her pocket. The shops were all open for her, workmen left their waiting on this ordinary extraordinary day. Her presence keeps us all willing working. It's a good trick. No doubt explains her hometown's impressively balanced budget. We went to Stockwell Road where she haggled with an elderly Portuguese man, two small boys watching in admiration. Walked Streatham High Road from Brixton Hill to the ice rink. Finally took a half-empty train to Borough Market and came home with our afternoon arms full of essential provisions. The birds are small and firm and clean. A small white feather floats down as I open the gate.

(Came home? I like that.) I will make you Toledo partridge with dark chocolate sauce.

I eat the chocolate, she grates it into my hand, hard and bitter, it wakens the edges of my tongue. She needs one glass of dry white wine for the dish. We keep back a glass each for ourselves and pour the rest at the base of the tree. Moisture enough for a London winter.

According to the old man in the high street shop, this bird laid fifteen eggs in one day. She was one of his finest, will do well for Catalan-style partridge, ten garlic gloves fat and pink, two dozen onions, not one of them larger than the O of your open mouthed love.

She peels each onion carefully, stripping back the finest layer of dry brown skin and exposing white flesh membrane beneath. She starts with a pearl-handled knife handed down from mother to daughter, then discards it in favour of the new one I bought last week at the Co-op, two small paring knives for the price of just one. By the fifth tiny onion her dark eyes are streaming. I stand at her left and catch tears for the stock.

Jewish partridge, we call this one, though probably the Arabs gave us the nuts, certainly the Romans brought the garum, and the clay pot belonged to my mother and her grandmother before. The meat is sweet and strong, I think perhaps you are too. They say partridges mate for life. You are a gardener and I am a cook, this should work well.

Dish follows dish, tiny bones picked and licked and sucked and cleaned. We eat small and delicate morsels across a whole day. The postman comes and goes, local bin men collect carefully piled recycling bottles and paper, black liner bags stuffed with onion skins and greasy paper napkins. I am so full. Full of her and of the day and all these months of waiting for her to come.

You do the dishes. I want to watch your Queen's Speech. My mother asked me to check it out.

Tidied house, street lights on, it's time now. We go outside. I walk barefoot on to a frosted ground, it must be truly cold for the suburb-heated grass to turn winter-crisp. I show her the shed, switch on the external lights. She is suitably impressed and turns to smile at my neighbour peering from behind tired nets. My neighbour has the gall to wave. The King of Spain's daughter pokes out her tongue. Maybe we won't be sharing next door's Boxing Day sherry after all.

Your tree is beautiful. As it should be. You are beautiful. As you should be. I am beautiful. But you knew that.

We consider dessert. A fresh golden pear, rice pudding with lightly grated nutmeg. But we are full, she and I, not greedy.

Sitting in the crystal palace of my shed, me and the King of Spain's daughter at my side, we talk of her journey and the heavy water of my knowing and if she thinks she will like brussels sprouts. I use my father's sister's recipe, cook them with chunks of salty bacon and stir in double cream at the very last minute. It's really not bad. Above us, reaching up to the glass ceiling and the pale orange sky of this old city, hang a silver nutmeg, a golden pear, and the wishbone of a partridge in a pear tree. The little tree is good to lean against, solid. You tell me your studies: Athena was worshipped as the mother of all pear trees. Perdix, one of Athena's sacred kings, became the partridge when he died – but in Badrinath, in the Himalayas, he himself was the Lord of the Pear Trees.

This tree is male-female, it carries us all.

Everyone always talks about the partridge, don't they? As if that were the point being made, the lone partridge, waiting hungrily for his life-long mate. No-one really thinks about the tree, how the precious fruit would grow, where the bird would land if the tree wasn't there. But I do, I planted it.

You planted it. It called me to you.

And now it holds us up.

SIREN SONGS

Ryan moved into the basement apartment with a heavy suitcase and a heavier heart. And the clasp on his suitcase was broken. And the clasp on his heart was broken, shattered, wide open, looted, empty. When Ryan moved into the basement apartment he was running away from a broken heart. Slow, loping run, limping run, with no home, job or car. Never a great idea for your beloved girlfriend to have an affair with your boss. The new apartment was cold, dark, dingy and not a little damp. It suited his mood, suited his budget, suited him. The bedroom had a small bed. Double certainly, but small double, semi-double. As if the bed itself knew what a mess Ryan and Theresa had made of things and kept its edges tight to remind him of where he had once been, the expansive stretch of past love. And where he was now.

Where Ryan was now was as bad as it had ever been. There had been other break-ups of course, Ryan was a grown man, he'd broken hearts, mended his own, broken again. But this one was different. He had loved Theresa, really-proper-ly-always. Love with plans, love with photo albums full of future possibilities, love made concrete by announced desire. Loved her still. And she had loved him too. But not enough. Just not enough. Not enough to wait while he worked too late, not enough to stay quiet when he shouted, open when he closed, faithful when he played first. Ryan had played first, but Theresa played better. Ryan lost. His fling was a one night forget-me-quick, hers was his boss and a fast twist of lust into relationship-maybe into thank you goodbye. Goodbye Ryan, hello new life.

Ryan did not blame Theresa, he blamed himself and his past experiences and his present ex-boss and the too-grand future he had planned for her in the lovely big apartment with the lovely big rent. The plans and hoping and maybes and mistakes first tempted and then overtook them both. Ryan believed in the future and Theresa was swamped by it. Either one could have been left out in the cold, in this case it was Ryan. Cold in damp sheets and small apartment and no natural sunlight and tear stained – yes, they were, he checked again, surprising himself – tear stained pillows. Salt water outlines on a faded lemon yellow that desperately needed the wash-and-fold his new street corner announced so proudly. And they'd get it too, these depression-comfortable sheets – once Ryan could make it back up the basement steps into the world. From where he lay now a decade didn't seem too long to hide. He lost some weight, bought some takeaway food, felt sorry for himself and listened to late-night talk shows. He followed the pattern. Waited it out. Morning becomes misery, becomes night and then another day, almost a week, and eventually, even the saddest man needs a bath.

Ryan stumbled his bleary, too much sleep, too little rest, too little Theresa, way through the narrow apartment. Touched grimy walls, glared at barred windows, crossed small rooms with inefficient lighting. But then he came to the bathroom. The Bathroom. A reason to take the place at his lowest, when the bathroom looked like a nice spot for razor blades and self pity. Ryan checked out just two apartments before he moved in to this one. The other was lighter and brighter but only had a shower, a power shower in a body-sized cubicle. Good size, it would take even his boy hulk bulk, but Ryan needed more. Needed to stretch into his pain, luxuriate in his sadness. And while heartbreak was pounding in his chest, Ryan's prime solace was the picture of himself in a bath of red, Theresa's constant tears washing his drained body. It was a tacky image to be sure, a nasty one, bitter and resentful and 'you'll be sorry when I'm gone'. Entirely childish, utterly juvenile, ludicrously self-pitying.

It worked for Ryan. He paid the deposit.

The glorious used-to-be-a-bedroom bathroom, highest window in the apartment, brightest room in the gloom. Bath with fat claw feet, hot and cold taps of shiniest chrome, towered over by an incongruously inappropriate gold shower attachment, smooth new enamel to hold his cold back and broad feet. A long, wide coffin of a bath, big enough for his big man's frame, deep enough to drown the grief. Maybe. Picture rail and intricate cornices and swirling whirl of centre ceiling rose, peeling and pock marked but still lovely, fading grand. Set high into the flaking plaster of the wall, was a grille. An old-fashioned cast iron grille; painted gold, picked out, perfect. The ex-owner had started to renovate the whole place, got as far as the bathroom plaster, the golden grille, and stopped. Dead. Heart attack while painting the ceiling. One corner remained saved from his endeavours, nicotine stained from the bath-smoking incumbents of years gone by. Ryan liked it, the possibility of staining. Considered taking up smoking. And then decided death-by-cancer would take too long. And he couldn't count on Theresa to rush back to him in a flurry of Florence Nightingale pity. (Though pity would do. Love had been great, but right now, ordinary old pity would do just fine.)

The first time he managed to get out of bed, away from the takeaway cartons, the television, the radio, the box-set DVD's and a wailing Lou Reed on a self-solace sound track (Ryan was in mourning, he hadn't stopped being a boy) he ran himself a bath, poured a beer and poured his protesting body into the welcoming water. Ryan was still picturing stones in his pockets and blades on his wrists, heavy stones, long vertical cuts, slow expiration. He had loved her. So very much. But he'd known nothing and the truth had all been proved to him in the end. Love's not enough, he wasn't enough, siren songs only last as long as the mermaid keeps her hair. Theresa had her hair cut a week before she dumped him. He thought it was for her new job. Seven days later he knew it was for her new man. James was a good boss, but he did have this thing about small women in sharp suits with short haircuts. Theresa had been wearing suits for a couple of months, lost a little weight, tightened up her act, her arse. Ryan noticed the clothes, the body, he read the signs, he just didn't know they weren't for him. The hieroglyphs of Theresa, road maps to a new desire.

There he was, in the bath with blades on his mind, but the water was hot and his skin was beginning to crinkle and in the comfort of the beautiful room, the only beautiful room, he thought – for the first time that week, for the first time since – that he just might make it through. Through this night anyway. And of course, truthfully, he wasn't going to cut his wrists. Not really, not even slightly-scratch in actress-poetess-girlie style. He was just picturing escape from heartbreak and the possibility of Theresa running her hands through his hair in the hospital, in the coffin. Just the possibility of her hands in his hair. Ryan likes his hair. Theresa loved it. Maybe he should cut it off and send it to her. She could make a rope of his hair and climb back to him. If she wanted to. She didn't want to. Theresa on his mind, in his hair. Theresa on his hands, time on his hands, nothing to do but think of her.

And then the singing started. Soft singing, girl-voice singing, slight held-under, under the breath, under the weather, under the water, coming from somewhere that was not this room but close. Coming through the steamy air, the curled damp hair, and into his water-logged ears. Coming into him. At first Ryan thought it was from next door. Another dank basement on either side of his, one more out back across the thin courtyard too. But it was three in the morning. And the left hand basement was a copy shop and the right hand one a chiropodist. No reason for middle night singing in either of them. Across the courtyard then. Past the rubbish bins, over the stacked empty boxes, around the safety-conscious bars and through the dirty glass. But although the window was high and bright it was also closed. Shut tight against the nameless terrors that inhabited his broken break-in sleep without Theresa. And this voice was floating in, not muffled through walls or glass, but echoing almost, amplified. And gorgeous. So very gorgeous. Just notes initially and then the mutation into song, recognisable song. Peggy Lee's 'Black Coffee'. Slow drip accompaniment from the now-cold hot tap. Gravelly Nico 'Chelsea Girls', Ryan soft-soaping his straining arms. Water turning cold and dead skin scummy to Minnie Ripperton 'Loving You'. And finally, letting the plug out and the water drain away from his folds and crevices while a voice-cracking last line Judy Garland saluted 'Somewhere Over the Rainbow'. Torch song temptress singing out the lyrics of Ryan's broken heart.

Ryan dried his wrinkled skin and touched the steam-dripping walls of the bathroom. Reached up to the golden grille. The grille which ran the height of all four apartments this old house had become. The grille that was letting in the voice. The voice that woke him up.

Ryan went to bed. Slept soundly. Arose with his alarm clock. (Midday, no point in pushing too far too soon.) Ate breakfast. (Dry cereal. Sour milk.) Tidied the apartment. (Shifted boxes and bags, some of them actually into the rubbish bin.) And, with a cup of coffee in hand, made a place for himself on the low wall opposite his building. He waited three hours. Buses passed him and trucks passed him, policemen talking into radios at their shoulders passed him. Schoolchildren passed him shouting and screaming at each other, entirely oblivious to Ryan's presence, his twenty years on their thirteen making him both invisible and blind. Deaf too. An old man passed him. Stopped, turned, wanted to chat. The weather – warm for this time of year, the streets – dirty, noisy, not like they used to be, young women – always the same. Ryan did not want to converse, did not want to be distracted from his purpose. So he nodded and smiled. Agreed to the warmth, shrugged off the noise, and couldn't help but engage with the women. The conversation took fifteen minutes, at most. In that time Ryan looked at the man maybe twice. But the man didn't think him rude. He thought him normal. The man was old after all. Didn't get many full-face chats any more. Nannies passed with squalling babies in buggies. Dog-walkers passed, pulled on by the lure of another thin city tree, the perfect lamppost. And one cat, strolling in the sunshine, glanced up at the sitting man and walked off smirking. Tail high in the air, intimate knowledge of Ryan's futile quest plain and simple. And laughable. Ryan knew it was laughable. But still, at least he was laughing.

At six in the evening, as the sun was starting to go down behind the building opposite, with a red-orange glint battering his eyes, a woman rounded the corner. She was young. Very young he thought. Too young to be living alone, surely? Scrabbling for keys in the bottom of her bag she walked right past him, turned abruptly, looked left and then right, crossed the road and walked up the steps to the door that let into the thin shared hallway and then the dark staircase to all three of the apartments above his. On her back she carried a backpack. In her backpack she carried a sleeping baby. The girl didn't look like she sang lullabies. Not often. And he'd heard no crying baby through the grille. He watched the lights go on in the front room of the top floor apartment, her blinds fall down the window, crossed her off his list. Shame. Too young, too mothering. Nice legs though.

He waited until midnight. It was time for dinner, supper, hot chocolate, bed. No-one else came. The young mother turned off her lights. The other apartments stayed empty and dark. He was cold, late spring day turned into crisp still-winter night. The woman in the top apartment needed to be careful of her window boxes. This hint of frost wouldn't do her geraniums any good. He could tell her that, when he found her, if he found her, if she sang the songs. He crossed the road and let himself into the hallway. Looked at the nondescript names on their post-boxes. Wondered which and who and went downstairs to the darker dark.

Ryan turned on every light in the apartment and ran a long bath, made a fat sandwich of almost-stale bread and definitely stale cheese (cleaning was one thing, proper shopping was definitely a distant second on the getting-better list) and lowered his chilled body into deep water, sandwich hand careful to stay dry. And just when he'd finished the first mouthful a door upstairs opened and closed. Then footsteps, more muffled. Another door. A third. He waited. Swallowed silently, chewed without noise, saliva working slowly on the wheat-dairy paste, teeth soft on his tongue. And then, again the water was cold, the food done, his arms just lifting water-heavy body from the bath, he heard it again. Singing through the grille, slow voice through the steam. Billie Holiday tonight. A roaring Aretha Franklin. And surprise finale theme tune to the Brady Bunch. Sweet voice nudged harsh voice twisted slow and smooth into comedy turn. He leapt even further then. Wet hand reaching to the grille, stronger determination to find her. Bed and alarm set for six am. Maybe she worked late, left early. He would too. Theresa was there, in his bed, in his head. But she wasn't hurting just now. Or not so much anyway. He must remember to buy some bread.

For a full week Ryan follows the same pattern. Gets up early, runs to the closest shop, buys three sandwiches, takes up his post opposite the house. The young mother comes and goes. Smiles at him at first and then gives up when he doesn't smile back, when his gaze is too concentrated past her, on the steps, on the windows, up and down the street. The old man passes every morning and every afternoon. Each time a new weather platitude, a new women truism. Ryan thinks he should be writing these down. The old man is clearly an expert in the ways of women, in the pain of women, the agony of women-and-men. Ryan changes his daily shifts by two hours each time. In twelve days he will have covered all the hours, twice. There are two other occupants of the house. One of them is the singer. He will find her. Theresa is fading. Still there, still scarring, but fading anyway. There is something else to think about, something else to listen to. It does help. Just as they always say so. Just as the old man says so. She left him a message yesterday morning, Theresa. And he only played it back five times. It was just a message, some boxes he'd left behind, when he planned to pick them up. She had nothing more to say to him. Even Ryan, even now, knew it didn't need playing more than five times.

And in the night, when he hasn't yet found the other two, caught the other two, followed their path from the door to hallway to specificity of individual window, while all he still knows for sure is the young, young mother, at night Ryan listens to the songs. Every night a new repertoire. Deborah Harry, Liza Minnelli, Patti Smith, Sophie Tucker, Nina Simone. A parade of lovelies echoing down the grille and into his steamy bathroom, through the mist to his eyes and ears, nose and mouth, breathing them in with the taste of his own wet skin, soap suds body, music soothing the savage beast in his broken breast. Ryan is really very clean. His mother would be proud. (She never much liked Theresa.)

The following Sunday, his eyes switching from one end of his street to the other, the old man just passed ('Never trust a pretty woman in high heels, either she'll trip up or you will'), about to start on his cinnamon bagel, he sees the door open on the other side of the street. The door to his maybe. A woman comes out. Middle aged, middle dressed, middle face between smile and scowl until she checks out the sky – it is sunny, she turns to smile. She is dressed to run. Locks the door behind her. (She has a key! She is one of them!) Makes a few cursory stretches, jogs down the steps, up again, down, stretch and away to the west end of the street. Ryan notes the time. Twenty minutes later she is back. Red faced, puffing hard, she is not running fast now, did not start off fast either, a slight lean to the left, lazy – or unaware – technique, bad shoes maybe, she stops at the steps. Sits, catches her breath. She takes off her shoes, removes a stone from one, replaces the sticky insole in the other. Runs fingers through her hair, red fingers, red face, faded red hair. She is his mother's age maybe. Ryan has a young mother, but she is his mother's age all the same. He is both disappointed and comforted. If she is the singer, then they are lullabies. Not the young mother lullabies to the wailing baby, but this older woman's lullabies to him. And they work. He is soothed. Would sleep in the bath but for the cooling water. She wipes sweat from her forehead. She is not beautiful, or particularly strong. She does not look like the singer of the songs. He watches her go inside and some minutes later follows. In the hallway, before descending the dark stairs to the basement (a lightbulb to replace, time to do it now, time and inclination) he catches the scent of her in the air. Woman older than him and more parental than him and sweatier than him and under all that a touch of the perfume she must have worn yesterday, last night. A stroke of the perfume she will wear again, proud to have been out and sweating, pleased with her slow progress towards firmness from age, flushed through with the pumping blood. Ryan scents all this in the hallway. And is happy to think of something not himself. Not Theresa. Brand new.

Then the songs change again. Britney and Whitney and Christine and Lavigne and other song lines he doesn't know the name of but knows what they look like, what they all look like, MTV ladies of the night, little bodies and lithe bodies with low pants or high skirts and bare midriffs, flashing splashing breasts beneath wide mouths with good smiles. They are up-tempo these songs and they don't soothe him any more, but they do excite him, awake him a little, remind him of what else and possibility and – when they rail and rant and proclaim and damn (mostly men, mostly boys, mostly life) – Ryan is re-minded he is not the only one. The identification with sixteen year old girls may be a little unusual, but he is not the only one. He is glad to be joined in his suffering-into-ordinary. Glad to have companionship in his ordinary-back-to-life. And, given the choice, he feels happier shouting along with the Lolitas than looking on with the old men. Ryan has never done letch very well. Naked and wet, he is all too aware of his own vul-nerability.

Ryan decides the third woman must be her. The She. The Singer. The One. Of course, either of the other two might be the singer, but he just can't see it. Not the young mother, tired as she seems to be from the baby and the college books she carries in and out every day. He knows they are college books. He has stopped and asked her. Helped her with them once, when the baby was screaming and she couldn't find her keys, and then another time too, when it was raining, summer rain, hot rain, and she needed to get the baby and her shopping and her books all inside at once. She asked him then, if he was always going to sit on the low wall opposite the house. If he didn't get bored. And Ryan wondered before he answered, what it must look like, him there, every day. How to answer her question without sounding insane. Or frightening. He told her that it was dark in the basement flat. He wanted to be out-doors. And she nodded, agreed. She used the fire escape herself quite often. Not that it was very safe. Not that she'd ever let the baby out there. But she needed to see the light sometimes, have it fall direct on her skin. And then she went upstairs. Grateful for his help with the books and the baby. And he smiled, realising he'd told her the truth.

It couldn't be the older woman either, his singer. Not that she didn't have a good voice. He'd heard her as she ran. She was getting better at running, faster, a cleaner stride. After the first few times listening to her own panting, she decided music would be easier and played tapes to keep herself going. Show tunes mostly. He heard her coming round the corner. Of course she had the slightly out-of-tune twist that comes from only hearing the sound in your ears and not your own voice as well, even then though, he knew she could sing. But she was a high, very soft, sweet soprano. Quite breathy. Perfectly nice but not strong. And the siren who sang down into his bath time sang with a low growl, a full-throated roar, a fierce, passionate woman's voice. This older lady was sweet, but she wasn't the one. She nodded at him now, as she had started to do when she got back to the house, wiped her brow, loosed the pull of her shoelaces. He heard the click of her tape recorder and the 42nd Street tap-skip-hum as she made her way up the steps.

Ryan nearly missed Carmella the first time. He'd almost

given up waiting. Was worried about what it looked like to be sitting there day after day. Was worried that the old man thought he was a fixture, that Ryan himself was a fixture like the old man. Was worried he needed to get a job. The redundancy package that left him without Theresa and without an apartment only left him with three months of feeling sorry for himself as well. And he'd wallowed through the first and now sat through another. He needed her to be the one. And, just as he was thinking now might be the right time to get up from the wall and walk to the shop and buy a newspaper, look for a job, there she was. Tall and slim and gorgeous. She'd been singing it last night, *Girl from Ipanema* in her swinging gait. Walking slowly down the stairs from her apartment, out of the gloom of the hallway to the glass of the front door. She stopped to check her mailbox. Long perfect nails, each one pretty pink. And Ryan knew this was her, she, the one, his singing angel. He started to get up from the wall, he didn't know what he would say but he knew he had to say it, must make a move, he'd lost Theresa, this wouldn't, couldn't happen again. She opened the door, he had his foot on the bottom step, she pulled the door back, he was looking up, she down, brown eyes met blue eyes, she smiled, he smiled, he started up, she started down. And kept coming, she fell on the second of five steps. Ryan decided it was meant. She fell into his arms, they tumbled to the pavement, arms and legs, hands and feet. When he sat up she was leaning against him, his right hand holding her left shoe. She smiled again.

'How kind. If you wouldn't mind?'

And he knelt to replace the shoe and knew with a startling clarity that this time, this one, this vision . . . was a man. A

beautiful, tall, delicious, perfect, angelic . . . man. Ryan replaced the size ten shoe and looked up.

'You may stand. If you wish.'

He did. Both.

'I'm Carmella. I live on the second floor. I'm a singer.'

'Yes.'

'I have to go. I'm sorry. I have a show.'

'Yes.'

'Thank you so much.'

She walks away. Ryan calls after her 'No. Thank you.'
Except that he doesn't. When he opens his mouth there is no
sound. She has stolen his sounds. And then Ryan laughs and,
gives in. Maybe the dream woman is not waiting for him on
the other side of the grille. Maybe she isn't really there. But she
has woken him anyway.

That night Ryan lies in the bath and waits for his siren. She
comes through the mist, singing of dreams and awakening.
Of perfect men and wonderful women. The next day, waiting
by the doorstep at the appropriate time for the appropriate
woman, Ryan asks each one of them out. He asks the young
woman to breakfast – on the way to the nursery, via the park,
then quick to college.

'Thanks, I'm really busy, but . . . yeah. OK. Thanks.
Anyway.'

The older woman agrees to lunch. An hour – and then
another half – grabbed from the office, damn them, why not,
why shouldn't she, after all?

'I'm never late back. Who'd have thought? Late back? Me!'

And then with Carmella to dinner. In her high heels and
short skirt and no need to catch when they fall.

The young mother is delighted and charmed and astonished to be treated as anything other than Jessie's mum. The older woman is delighted and charmed and astonished to be treated to anything by a younger man of Ryan's age. And Carmella who is Colin is delighted and charmed and astonished to be treated generously by such an obviously good-looking, obviously straight man. (And it's such a long time since Ryan thought of himself as good looking that he too is astonished, charmed, delighted.)

There is eating and drinking. They are nice, good to do. There is music and singing. Of course there is singing. Time passes. Because it does. Ryan feels better. Because he can. Life goes on. It cannot go back. The baby grows, the young woman takes on another year at college. The older woman enters a six-kilometre fun run. It takes her ninety-eight minutes to complete the course and Ryan waits for her at the finishing line. Carmella gets another gig, a better show, learns a whole new repertoire. And buys a new wig, lovely shoes. Ryan gets a job, one he thinks he might like, where the office is high above the street and floor to ceiling windows let in the light missing from his home. He begins to date again: good dates and inappropriate dates and wildly misjudged dates. And then the right one comes along when he isn't even looking, when he has a paper to be worked on this minute, before lunch, right now. Passes his desk. Stops for a chat. Stays for coffee. Ryan has met another woman. Carmella sings into the night. A right woman, a good woman. Carmella sings clean through the morning. And Ryan tries harder and the new woman tries harder and it works. Carmella tries out her opera routine, segues into slow ballad, then fast rock, hint of lullaby calm. Ryan and the new woman are giving it a chance. For now, for as long as it can, for as long as they will. As is the way of these things.

And, in the basement apartment with the deep claw-foot bath and the sound of possibility echoing down the golden grille, Ryan and his new love Chantal bathe happily ever after. More or less.

THE GILDER'S APPRENTICE

Whenever the gilder finished a task he took a moment to himself before allowing anyone else to see the piece, be they his own apprentices or the person who had commissioned the work. He would tell the apprentices to step back, ten, fifteen paces. Then he would bring his hands together, one on top of the other – the left hand always went down first – touching the piece very closely, yet not touching it either, so that not a lifeline or fingerprint whorl might be seen on the finished article. He told his apprentices he did it to feel the gold, that they needed to learn to feel the gold moving beneath their fingers, feel it settling on the wood or the clay or the iron, feel it becoming part of whatever it covered. He held his hands close enough to touch the warmth of the gold, for the gold to touch him. When he was done his cheeks would be drawn, his face pale, and he needed to take a minute, to breathe deeply. Then the work was handed over, and the next job begun.

The gilder was much in demand. When he handed back the frame, unveiled the gate, showed the precious jewelled box that had been restored to an even finer state than hoped, people would comment on the depth of the gold, its richness, its warmth. Always its warmth. In fifty years of working the gilder had known difficult times, of course, but there was still a queue for his skill. He was known to supervise his apprentices closely, and their work was also highly rated, but a premium was paid for his own craftsmanship, for the knowledge that his hands had been placed/not-placed on the piece at the very end.

The gilder began as an ordinary carpenter's boy, an unsuccessful carpenter's boy at that. There was nothing in dovetail joints or mitre cuts, in chalk lines or plumb lines, in frames or lathes that excited him. He was a good enough worker and although he didn't much care for the job, his was a time with little work and less security; to work was better than not, to bring home a wage was always welcome, what with his father broken since the war and three younger children at home, his mother's face grey with worry and the reflection of other people's dirty laundry. He would work out the years of his indenture and being a carpenter would be good enough.

Except that it wasn't enough. He got by, brought in enough, made a living – just. And the day came when just wasn't enough. He wanted more. He wanted special and good and his own. He wanted passion.

He tried to speak to his mother about it but she was too busy filling the looping line with the neighbours' washing and the neighbour's neighbour's washing, as a plain stew bubbled on the stove for her husband's tea.

She looked up from the washing basket, held someone else's clean dirty laundry out to her son and said, 'Passion? You don't know the half of it lad, you don't want to ask after passion. This is what passion gets you. Ask your Dad.'

And so he asked his father and his father, speech

slurring from a mouth half-opening, one eye half-closed, always, against light too bright, any light, the other glass and unseeing, his father answered,

'Passion? Passion got me this – ' and he pointed to the foot that was blown off. 'Passion got me this –' and he held up a shaking arm, always shaking.

'Passion, a cause, desire running hotter than my stupid head lost me an eye. You don't want passion, boy. You want safe. Now get off to work and be thankful you've a job to go to and a body whole enough to do it.'

And yet.

He tried to be thankful. Under his boss's supervision – one boss, two apprentices, three jobs – he put in a new loft for one of those couples in the terrace where everyone had a new loft. Then he extended a side return for another family in another terrace where everyone had an extended side return. And the clients always exclaimed both their pleasure at the work and their shock at the price. They always thanked him, but they also shook their heads as they wrote out the cheques, offered chunks of cash for less, offered VAT-off ready money. They were grateful, but not that grateful. And he understood the feeling. He was grateful for the job, but not that grateful. He could see when he'd made a good job of his work, completed on time, costs just to the edge of budget, cleaning up after him as he went; the boss insisted on that, nothing made the owners happier than seeing the work done and everything clean and tidy – as if the work had never been done, as if the new things had always been there. The clients wanted new and at the same time they wanted it to look as if the workers had never been there. But the apprentice wanted to do more.

Wanted to make a difference, wanted to cause change, wanted his work to shine. Wanted it, and went home, to the family where there was no loft conversion, no extended side return, just three younger siblings and a sad-eyed mother, and a bitter, shaking father, and a wage at the end of the week. Be thankful lad, be thankful.

The apprentice wasn't thankful. He was bored. And as the boredom set in more strongly, so did his tiredness, and the tiredness turned to a lethargy and the lethargy to a depression and although, by rights, he had nothing to worry about, to be sad about – it wasn't his body that was broken, his job that was lost, his child missing out – the apprentice just couldn't shake the sadness. The sadness of every day being not quite enough.

And then.

His boss noticed and sent for him.

'Look here, we can't all have what we want, we can't all be captains of industry, high-flyers, the makers of difference, we can't all be that. Someone has to stay down here, on the ground – holding down the ground. It would all fly up if some of us weren't down here, you know that, don't you lad?'

He didn't, but the apprentice appreciated the smile in the boss's voice, the attempt at levity, appreciated the older man trying to lift him up while pinning him firmly down, and he took the next job handed out and he determined, this time I will do my best. And I won't mind if the owners want it to be a job that becomes unnoticed. I will know, I will note it, I will do this job as if it were a job of joy forever.

It was a job of dust for five days. Every floor, every window, every door to be sanded, hot-air-gunned, blasted, stripped back to the original wood. (The original wood the Victorians had never meant to be shown as wood, but never mind, the apprentice didn't bother telling them that.) He smiled. He thanked the couple and pulled up carpets and closed doors behind him and went to work. After the stripping and sanding and revealing came the waxing and varnishing. Another five-day job of re-doing to undo the undoing.

It was Saturday morning, the young couple were downstairs. She, six months pregnant, looking forward with every passing week to her maternity leave and a nesting instinct she didn't yet feel, hoped she would feel. He, first-time father checking books and figures, online statements and paper files, scared to be dad. Both excited and worried, neither fully honest with each other about their fears, preoccupied.

The apprentice was working on the last room. The young couple's bedroom. The other rooms had been exclaimed over, praised, and then – varnish dry, wax polished – the doors were closed off to protect them from the prying eyes of the apprentice who had looked into every nook and cranny, had counted more skin cells and lost hairs in the folds between floorboards than he could remember. Never mind. And, if he didn't feel much cheerier, any less tired, any less hopeless, he could at least say he'd done his best. Given giving it a go a go.

And then. The loose floorboard by the pregnant woman's side of the bed. The floorboard he had fiddled with while sanding, promising to return with claw hammer and new nails before varnishing. That floorboard. He slipped the claw in carefully and began to lift, gently gently, bad timing now to chip, splinter or crack. He felt the slightest resistance, almost as if something were pushing the two-pronged claw of the hammer away, something lightly, kindly, saying no, and then the board gave and lifted, it sat up to welcome him. And beneath the board, in the recess between this floor and that ceiling, in the in-between, there was a mechanism. A slightly rusty, very dusty, spring-loaded mechanism. It was the bell to call the maid who must once have lived in this house. A maid who might have worked for a couple just like these two, a maid who blacked the grates and emptied the slops and scrubbed the front step and polished the floors and perhaps even left a casserole warm in the oven when she went back, once a fortnight, to her own family's smaller, meaner home. The apprentice shook his head. The young couple, a few years older than he was, owned an ordinary three-bedroom terrace. He couldn't see himself ever having the deposit for something like this, not even round here, where gentrification would only ever reach the edge of the old council estate. Not even round here. And so it must always have been. A young couple, with a few rooms, in a newly-built Victorian terrace, in an unfashionable part of the city where the railway ran. And they could afford a maid. On his hands and knees, peering into the in-between, the apprentice thought about chance and birth and luck and good fortune and just how it was. How it is.

Even so, he called the owners.

'Look at this. A bell, for calling your maid. Imagine that. A maid.'

And the young woman said she wouldn't mind if it was a bell for a night-nanny, she could imagine getting used to that.

And the young man shrugged and asked if they needed to get it taken out and could the apprentice do it and would it cost more or could he put the floorboard back safely and leave it there and just get on with the job?

There was a distinct tone in the bloke's voice that the apprentice was wasting time when he could be waxing, varnishing, breathing in dust and fumes.

They left the room, shaking their heads over what had been and what was now, but only a little, they had too much what would be to worry about, and they left the apprentice to get on with it.

And then. Against his better judgment, because the apprentice knew he should never ring a bell he didn't want answered – he rang the bell. Quietly, softly. And nothing happened, but a dull thud, not even a real tinkle, too much dust and rust in the mechanism, the spring too old to bounce back. Nothing happened. The apprentice dusted down the bell, vacuumed away a century of small things fallen between the cracks, rang the bell – again softly, again quietly – one more time, and then he replaced the floorboard. Hammered and nailed into place, smoothed, varnished, finished. As if it had never been done, never been rung.

That night the apprentice sat in the pub with his mates. They talked about football, rubbish. Telly, rubbish. Women, not rubbish, but not easy, definitely not easy. And work. Rubbish. The apprentice's friends talked about this girl in the office, and that bloke who sent out the cabs, and the old girl in accounts and the old bloke in shipping and each one of them had horror stories of the Monday to Friday, Monday to Saturday for those like the apprentice, and each one of them laughed at his mates' stories and told his own like it was high drama, and each one of them, having told the tale, moved on. Back to football, still rubbish. And because they had known each other since school, since before they were even teenagers, and because they met every Friday night and said the same things every Friday night, and because they knew how it was, at home, all the lads went easy on their mate the apprentice when it came time to buy his round. They liked him, he was a good bloke, things were bad now, had been bad for a while, things would get better eventually. And because they were his mates the apprentice let them go easy on him and didn't make a fuss or insist on paying his way, he just went up to the bar and ordered the half dozen half pints.

He carried over four half pints, went back to the bar for the last two and a few bags of crisps. A gesture, and welcome. His hands full, he turned and bumped smack into an old man.

Shit. Sorry.

The apprentice swore first, the old man swore next, they said sorry at the same time. Smiled. The apprentice looked down and, where he expected beer on his shirt, lager on the old man's jumper, where he had felt the swell of the half-pint glasses, had caught the sway of moving liquid, the old man was reaching out, almost touching the glasses, the crisps, just. And the beer did not spill. And his mates did not take the piss. And the crisps were eaten. It was a good night.

When last orders came around the apprentice got up to go. Those with their office jobs told him to sit back down again, but the apprentice was adamant. Saturday working was bad enough, with a hangover it was hell. He held up his hand, smiled round the table, and walked from the bar with shouts of loser ringing behind him. He heard it every Friday, had done since he started his apprenticeship. He was beginning to wonder if maybe they were right.

Late Friday night, winter, cold outside after the warmth of friends and fumes in the pub. The apprentice zipped up his jacket, pulled the collar up around his ears, started down the road on his walk home.

'Lad. Wait up. Lad.'

He turned. The old man was standing in the doorway.

'Do you mind? If I walk a way with you? I don't like to walk on my own, winter, icy roads.'

The apprentice looked at the old man. He had to be eighty if he was a year, he wasn't going to mug him, and if this was the way old blokes came on to young men these days, well, it wasn't going to turn him gay either.

'I'm turning right at the end of the High Street. Any good to you?'

'Yes. Yes it is.'

The old man nodded and they walked together.

As they walked the old man asked the apprentice about himself. The apprentice told him about his work, the relentless days of it, how even though he felt he was doing good things for people, nice things, there was no shine to his days. The old man nodded, he too had once worked in that way. But he told the apprentice something else, something that made the apprentice laugh and shake his head and say I wish. I wish.

'You don't believe me? Look.'

They were almost at the end of the High Street, the apprentice was about to turn left, the old man right, and as they stood there, in the cold night, at the dark end of the long street, the old man reached into his pocket and pulled out a tin. It was a tobacco tin, the kind the apprentice's grandfather used to keep his tobacco and rolling papers in. The apprentice smiled to see it and in the dark night he caught an image of his grandfather, long gone now, another man, like this one, whose work had made him happy.

The old man put arthritic fingers to the lid of the tin and pulled carefully, with a slight twisting motion, a twisting that the apprentice thought seemed odd for a rectangular tin, and yet the lid eased off anyway.

He held out the tin to the apprentice.

'Do you know what this is?'

The sodium light washed everything out to yellows and greys, but even so, the apprentice thought he knew what he was looking at.

'Gold leaf?'

The old man nodded.

'I was a gilder by trade, for sixty years, more. I can teach you – if you like? It's slow learning, takes time, but they'll notice your work all right, I can promise you that. Look.'

And the old man carefully pulled a fine sheet of gold from the tin, he held it up to the streetlight and then, turning to the apprentice, he winked.

'Over here I think.'

The apprentice followed the old man towards a parking meter.

'These'll all be gone soon.'

'They're replacing them with ones you pay for on your mobile.'

'Fine if you have a mobile.'

The apprentice shrugged. 'Or a car.'

The old man pulled a little vial of oil from his pocket, and another of gum, he smeared both on the meter, working it with his index finger. He then held the gold leaf out to the timer on the parking meter, sizing it up, and with fingers that moved carefully and deliberately despite their twisted joints, he placed the gold on the parking meter, stretching and smoothing it out, sliding his thumb along the metal and making the gold one with the meter until he had completely covered the face of the parking meter.

'There,' he said. 'Now the time can't tick away.'

The apprentice stared at the meter. It was clean and sharp and bright, it was warm with a red gold that held light even as it reflected it.

'Yes,' he nodded, 'please. Teach me how to do that.'

The old man staggered then, gasping for breath, he reached out to grab the apprentice's arm.

'Are you ok?'

'Just a little faint, that's all. Not as young as I used to be, the blood doesn't flow as well as it did.'

The apprentice offered to walk the old man home, and the old man offered to take the apprentice on.

In the morning the apprentice walked the long way to work, so he could go past the parking meter. And it had not been a dream and the meter was shining. In the thin winter sunlight it was the warmest thing on the street.

And so the apprentice began his second apprenticeship. While he still worked six days a week for his carpenter boss, he now worked two evenings a week and every second Sunday with the gilder. He started with oil gilding and slowly, careful-ly, built up to water gilding. He started with alloys of copper or brass or zinc and then, eventually, because he was a quick student and because he worked hard, the old man gave him his first sheet of twenty-four carat gold to work with. He worked it well.

Time spent with the old man was a pleasure, and the apprentice found that because he looked forward to his Tuesday and Thursday evenings, to his Sunday mornings, his other days became more pleasurable too. He started to add effects to the work he did as a carpenter, offering a small flourish of gilt here, a touch of gold there, and when they were brave enough to say yes, the clients liked what he gave them, liked that he left his mark. But even though he worked all the spare hours he could with the old man, as the days of his first apprenticeship began to draw to a close, he never could make his own gilding look as rich, as deep, as the old man's. The apprentice's gold was always lighter, yellower. The old man's gold glowed warm, shot through with a deep richness that was almost red. And the apprentice wanted to know how to do that.

He asked the old man.

The old man frowned, ran a hand over his face, nodded, smiled.

'Yes,' he said, 'I think it's time.'

He told the apprentice about the first gold mines in Egypt and Nubia, about the uses of gold in medicine and science, gold for food and gold for the gods, of the gold waiting in the vast oceans, and then, when he had told him the first seventy-eight secrets of gold, he told him the seventy-ninth.

And when he had told him the seventy-ninth secret, he showed him how to do it. The apprentice watched, amazed, excited, understanding, quiet. When he had given it all up, the old man thanked the apprentice, and said he really needed to sleep, he was tired, it was time.

As he stood at the door, ready to leave, the apprentice asked the old man, 'Why me? Why did you decide to share the secret with me?'

The old man smiled and said, 'You called me.'

'I did?'

'You rang the bell.'

And the apprentice felt again the rusty spring mechanism beneath his fingers, the dust covering the old servants' bell.

'You rang the bell and that night, in the pub, you said sorry to an old bloke who bumped into you.'

The apprentice looked at his mentor and friend, saw the man's pale face, even his lips now drained of blood.

'You bumped into me on purpose?'

'You looked like you needed a hand.' The old man closed his eyes, 'You should go now lad, I'm very tired.'

The apprentice helped the old man to his chair, looked around the workroom for what he knew would be the last time, took in the gilt-backed chair, the gilt-edged books, the gold-tipped pencils and pens, the gold-backed mirror, all the things the old man had shown him how to make lovely, make shine, and he saw they were all a deeper gold now, a redder gold.

He wished the old man good night and he thanked him. But the old man was already gone.

All that was very many years ago, and the apprentice is an old man himself now, his hands are arthritic and he must work even more carefully, deliberately. His unhappy father and tired mother are dust, the brother and sisters all grown up. There is a wife, and children too, a wife who wears a ring of warm red gold. They found each other late in life and took a chance on pleasure. He likes to say the children – the same age as his little brother's grandchildren – keep him young. He likes to say it, but it isn't true.

The apprentice has his own lads working for him, girls too – times have changed, but techniques haven't. He shows them the tricks of the trade, the dovetail joints and mitre cuts, the sanding and polishing, smoothing and finishing. Sometimes he teaches gilding too. But only if they are hungry for the difference, for the shine.

One day he will share the trick that the old man showed him. He will whisper the method for making gold richer, redder; the passing of real gold, true red gold, from hand to object, from lifeline to piece, real gold made precious by his almost-touching of it, made precious by his blood in it, his life in it.

It is tiring, literally pouring himself, his life, his life blood, into everything he does. But he does love the job.

UNCERTAINTIES AND SMALL SURPRISES

'THERE ARE UNCERTAINTIES,' he says, leaning over her in the near empty carriage, 'Uncertainties and small surprises to be had in an underground journey.'

He sits beside her. She smiles politely, buries her head deeper in her old copy of *Time Out*. Reads the letters page. Twice. It does no good. He starts again, smiling now.

'Take for example, the Northern Line train travelling south.'

She begins to wish she hadn't. The two city gentlemen, misplaced in the far corner of a late night tube, shuffle their newspapers, glare at her and at the chattering man for disturbing them, say nothing. This man has a point to make, about trains and other matters. He goes on to make it.

'The notice board says 'see front of train'. The train, of course, says nothing. It is not after all, Thomas the Tank Engine. It does not have the luxury of a voice over by Ringo Starr. Anyway, you decide to take your fate into your own hands. You board the train intending to travel to Victoria to meet your mother at the coach station and . . .' here he places his hand on hers for emphasis, her arm stiffens, she waits for his hand to move away. It goes nowhere. His grip is tight. He cares about his subject. The train takes a corner a little too quickly and he lurches once more into his discussion.

'And this is the good bit – it doesn't matter which line the train takes. Charing Cross or City Branch. It simply doesn't matter. You will not know what to do until you pass through the ghost of Mornington Crescent. Or not. Of course it is quicker to go to Euston on the Bank Line. You need only to cross the platform there. A few steps to the train you want. And those Victoria Line trains are so very regular.'

Far more regular than the beating of her heart which has gathered momentum in pace with his speech and is now racing at a speed of knots, charged up with adrenaline. Fearful adrenaline. And, if she is honest, which she always is, a tiny breath of excitement too.

Her arm loses its tension and she nods as if giving him permission to continue. He smiles.

'And that is where the small surprise lies. If you have plenty of time and can enjoy the fretful unease of at least six people in the carriage when they realise they are on the wrong side of the Northern Line – you can have a pleasant and enjoyable five minutes in what is usually described as one of the most nightmare of underground journeys. You don't know what's coming but it doesn't matter. You will arrive at the same destination no matter what route you take. How often can you say that in life, eh? Of course, it only works if you're not in a hurry.'

She makes a leap of judgement and from observing becomes participant.

'Are you often not in a hurry?'

He looks at her, startled that she has joined him. This is new and unexpected. A small surprise.

'Well, no. Almost never. Still, I imagine it's good when it happens.'

She nods, folds the magazine in half and puts it back in her bag.

'Oh, it's always good when it happens.'

He moves his hand from her arm. He is not used to conversation. Does not invite conversation. He sits beside her and shuffles in his seat, his back sweaty against the dark stained covers. Dirty tunnel wind whips across his face and he looks at her, sideways through the cultivated lank fringe that flops over his left eye.

'I'm sorry. I don't think I understand. When what happens?'

'A surprise.'

The train slows. they have been though Euston, Kings Cross, the Angel. The men with neatly folded newspapers have left them alone, plunging into the dark routes home, excuses close at hand. This is Old Street. She stands. Now she leans over him.

'This is my stop. Do you want to come?'

The train has shuddered itself into the station, the doors open.

'It's an uncertainty, isn't it? Do you want to come?'

She is more insistent. She likes this. Likes to lean over him. She can smell his hair, could kiss his forehead if the train jolted her forward only two centimetres. 'Quickly. Yes or no?'

Three lads roll into the carriage. They are drunk and loud. Louts. Young men frighten him. Even though he is a young man himself. There are no uncertainties with young men. He prefers to be surprised. Young men frighten her too. In packs. She knows how to take care of the singular. She puts her hand on his. 'Coming?'

He stands and they jump from the train as the doors begin to slam shut. She leads him quickly up stairs and through the empty passages and on to the escalator. They emerge into the open den entrance hall, rabbit warren alleyways leading out in circles to dark midnight. It was the last train south. He will not get home now. She runs up the escalator two moving steps at a time, he is out of breath trying to keep up. Her boots are DM's, shiny black patent leather. Small. She is small. Even in the running and out of breath, he acknowledges she would look silly with bigger feet. Like Minnie Mouse. This girl is small. He senses she is no mouse. This is an adventure. He is running up the steps like a man in a movie. He is tall and striding and she will take him home and make love to him and feed him and he will sleep in her caress and wake in a London that is not rain swept and winter dirty. He sees all this as they pass one after the other through the same ticket barrier. He looks over her little, narrow shoulders and sees all of this. He is seeing things.

Outside it is wet, cold after the suffocating recycled warmth of the tube. He shivers in the wind. She turns and laughs, grabs his hand again.

'Should have brought a coat, shouldn't you?'

Hers is red. Red wool he thinks, with black velvet collar and cuffs. It looks expensive. But she doesn't. There is something too sharp about her to look wealthy. And besides, she is leading him through alleyways, down dark streets. These houses are not tall white painted georgians. She is leading him to a council block. Up stairs, dark, lit by broken lights and reflected dirty puddles. She wouldn't live four floors up in a council block off Old Street if she was wearing a real wool coat. He thinks all this in the time it takes her to grab her keys from the bottom of her overfull bag and let them in. They walk down a short, blue painted passage. She shows him into the sitting room, turns on the light. It is normal. There is a view through the windows, she pulls the curtains against the distant lights of the city and the far more present tower block looming opposite. The room is small now and quiet, except for the remote thump of a too loud bass on a neighbours stereo. There is a rug in front of the gas fire. A tiger skin rug. With head and staring, wide open eyes. The tail and ears are moth eaten.

'Like my cat?'

He laughs.

'It looks like it got a bit of a shock.'

'One of your small surprises?'

'Maybe. Do tigers deal in journeying uncertainties?'

She shrugs her shoulders.

'This one did.'

In the shrug, her autumn red hair lifts with the black velvet collar of her coat. He glances at the nape of her neck. Likes the look of it, her pale skin, and then looks back at the rug.

'It's cool, I suppose. But it's a bit old isn't it? A bit ravaged. You could pick up something nice from Camden Market. There's those great sun and moon rugs. Everyone's got them.'

Her smile is compassionate, knowing.

'Yes. They have. I'll see. I'll think about it. Turn on the fire.

I'll make us a nice cup of tea.'

He had thought sex. At the least a quick snog, a fumble. But tea? He didn't think that women with tiger skin rugs drank tea. Even small women with narrow shoulders and wide hips. He frowns and looks at her.

'No beer?'

Her smile is still there.

'Leave it to me. It'll be a surprise.'

In the kitchen her hands are deft. The tea is to be ginger and honey. Warming with lots of soft brown sugar, lemon and a large dash of whiskey. She is still unclear as to why she has brought him here. Not sure what she means to do with him. Not sure why she did it in the first place. She hears him walking around her sitting room. He will be looking at the books, the pictures, the photos. Her sister, her ex-lover. While the kettle boils she removes her coat and boots. The kettle begins to whistle and in its admiring glance she takes off her dress, tights, Marks and Spencer's matching knickers and bra. A softer and babier pink than she feels. She pours bubbling water into the pot, a drop breaks out and splashes her naked stomach, she licks her finger and smooths the tiny burn with her own cool saliva. She arranges the tray with heavy mugs and tea-cosied pot, a plate of tiny sweet japanese biscuits and four thin slices of lemon.

She enters the sitting room with her offering.

He is on the floor by the fire. Going through her record collection. She has not yet graduated to cd's. He had expected to hear her boots return and is surprised by padding feet. He looks up at her. He is surprised.

'Oh. Yeah. I mean . . . wow! Great!'

In his exposition on the uncertainties of tube travel she had thought him almost eloquent. It had helped her to take his hand, offer herself. Now, in the face of her flesh, he has lost his words. She hopes he will rediscover the power of speech. She kneels on the rug, pours tea, adds lemon, a little more whiskey. She hands him his drink. She waits for composure to return to him. She had thought that making herself naked in her own home would grant him some of the power he'd thrown away as he came through the door. She had also thought that it might just give her more power. She wasn't sure which would happen. You never can tell until the clothes are off. Another small uncertainty.

She takes the Joni Mitchell album from him and they drink hot tea with a free man in Paris. He is not sure if he is a free man tonight but the tea has woken and refreshed him, it is whiskey heavy and ginger invigorating like the whiskey macs his father made him when they'd come in late from a cold night on the terraces. His mother clucked her disapproval. The young woman in front of him smiles assent. He leans to kiss her and finds that the soft peck on her mouth is biting back at his lips, cheek, tongue. Their mouths taste of the same bitter-sweet liquid. His shirt, damp from tube sweat, rain wet and nearly dried by the gas fire is damp again, sweat running from his armpits. He smells like travel and the beginnings of sex. Her nose wrinkles. She is still uncertain. Knows what to do next but not what to do after.

He is quickly naked. There is art in the removal of patent leather DM's, slowly drawing the shoelace through the silver eyelet holes. There is no art in the removal of thin wet shirt, old trainers, ripped jeans. They kneel opposite each other. The tea things to her left. Her narrow shoulders and wide hips swing towards him. He is not unaware that there is a certain ceremonial touch to all this, he just doesn't know what the ceremony is for.

In the hot moment of fucking, she looks down at him. His eyes shut tight beneath her kisses. She has done the next thing. The kissing. And done the next thing. The biting. And the next. The tracing of his collarbones under his thin blue veined skin. The kissing of his nipples, the kissing of his cock. They have been polite and quiet, taking it in turns to do the next thing and the next. They have maintained the order and the pattern that is expected even from a fuck picked up on the tube between Camden Town and Euston. And now they are here, in the fuck, the tiger is smiling at her and the young man's temples are throbbing above tightly shut eyes, all his energy, his life, pitched into doing that next thing. He would call out her name but he doesn't know it. She nods to the tiger, shakes her head clear of thought and joins this man in the moment of body where the only uncertainty is in when and the smallest surprise is the quiet 'oh' of after. Tired and finished he rolls himself into her and she strokes him to sleep.

He sleeps easy and fast.

She leaves him curled on the tiger rug and takes the tray back to the kitchen. On the draining board is the small paring knife she used to cut the lemon slices. The knife cuts sharply into his throat, his eyelids flutter as if they would wake and warn him but it is too late, he feels the acid of the lemon juice as he drowns in the gurgling blood and hiss of escaping air. She is glad she is naked, she would not want to stain the green velvet dress. The tiger is bloodied but that doesn't matter. The tiger is old. She has needed a new rug for some time. He said so, didn't he? She is finished in a couple of hours. Goes to the bathroom and showers with the plastic shower attachment. Her father had promised to put in a real shower but died before he had time. She could have done it herself, an easy enough job according to the cute boy in the hardware shop, but she'd never wanted to acknowledge to her father, even in death, that he was expendable. Besides, the shower attachment, in ugly grey plastic has a certain seventies, retro charm.

She goes to bed alone, Joni Mitchell in her head, his kiss on her breath.

In the morning she wakes bright and early. Climbs out of bed and pulls on her gym gear. She must do something to build up these narrow shoulders. Run more, swim more. Be more with her body. The morning is fine and clear, last night's rain has left a sharp clean city behind it. On her way out of the flat she peeks into the sitting room. He is lying in front of the fire, in a pool of pale winter sunshine. A man skin rug. With a look of surprise on his face.

STICK FIGURES

THE STICK IS the most glorious signifier. Yes, she has been far more ill than this. Standing on death's door, suitcase in her hand, a songbook compendium of how close to the very far. Or other times, not physically ill but worse, heartsick. The pumping organ of possibility shattered and bleeding and inexplicably pumping still. Pushing through the life-giving blood regardless, when all she wanted from life-giving was to give it away. She has been far more far gone than this. She has sat in the bright-lit pit of despair and known darkness was never coming back to offer fake-death solace. Today though, she is the victim of average muscle spasm, ordinary back ruination. After weeks of too much fun, at the end-of-joy-times, she walks with a stick.

The stick is useful, last night she used two to climb the stairs. One her own, the other a hand-me-down legacy from her grandmother's death, the stick turned chalice, its host of heavy memories was so full. Climbing the stairs with those two was a hazardous ascent, suburban K2. Today she uses just the one, her own. A painted walnut stick, straight and solid but light, plastic handle ending in a dragon-head mould, a gift on her thirtieth birthday. Joke gift, comedy present, and yet so useful. Too useful. Too damn necessary. But that is just the background, the how-to of getting here. And it is the point of now that matters, more than the past passing of arrival.

Now, she stands on the threshold of the foyer, helped from the car, the partner-as-driver speeding off to find free parking in time for the drinks and chocolate purchases that are the only way to get through these next hours. And the stick-bearer is left alone for the first time in seven days. She takes a trembling step. The steps are trembling, the pain is real. And she holds the stick before her. It is not noticed at first, the lights are dim at the entrance, the queue for programmes and sweets lengthy, the milling children stand in the way of the dragon's head she clasps surprisingly comfortably in her right hand. But then with a step-limp-step she moves into the body of the room, the double size ceiling, a mezzanine of watchers ready to look. Just in case, just in case she is someone who matters. She is not. But something about her does. And the stick sweeps all before it. It creates a path. Watchful fathers pull heedless children from before her, teenage girls turn shuffled backs, old ladies offer sympathetic glances. Sympathetic and not a little curious. She is not an old lady. But she is surely ill.

The stick is a wand, conjuring stories in those around her. The old men bless their good fortune and assume the worst. She has been struck down by an incurable disease, she is not long for this world. The women try not to look her in the eye, not to know too much. The teenagers do their best to ignore her. They are out of place anyway in such a theatre foyer, brought along by over-eager godparents or fissured-family obligation, forced here by tickets and purchases proving they are still unaware that while the child is no longer a child, he or she also not ready for the step to adulthood that might make the Christmas treat again a joy. The semi-young and still-young are not yet ready to process the fear that seeing another woman in pain stirs in them. She carries an obvious signifier of bodily decay but she is not that much older than them. Twenty years perhaps, and though those twenty years seem many more decades, even the most callow recognise her clothes are younger than their parents' dress, her hair is a better cut and colour. And yet she carries that stick. She is a symbol of death in their post-Christmas glitz and it is not right they should have to look at her. The teenage boy passes his friend another bottle of the illegally bought Bacardi Breezer with which his step-father hopes to ingratiate himself and they turn from the dangerous sight the stick-bearer offers. The limping woman is a witch to make them think of these things.

She continues her slow hop march through the room and now there is a teenage girl looking at her. She looks like a teenage girl. That is, she looks with the manner of a teenage girl – half defiant stare, half embarrassed snigger. She cannot help herself, her face simply forms into the sneer of semi-shame. Shame for the woman walking with a stick and shame at her own more than passing interest. This is the look that has not yet perfected itself into a mask of adulthood. It does not entirely understand how to lie, covers itself with squint and sneer and giggle and wide-eyed wonder that a body could do so much damage to its walker. Not that this girl does not fight her own bloody body battles, not that her own skin and flesh and not-enough-bone has not betrayed her often enough – but that a body should do so this publicly. The teenage girl endures agonies both silent and loud-voiced but despite her constant cries – or perhaps because of their very open nature – she is also perfectly aware that most of what makes her cry and lie awake at night is not all that obvious. She has read the books and seen the educational videos they provide at school, she may have anorexic body, but she does not have anorexic head. She is often in pain and at the same time she absolutely knows that in the eyes that look out of other heads, she is perfectly gorgeous and young and fine. There is nothing about her – even with the thin arms and legs – to suggest to the general public that she might be harmed. This girl lives in the real world after all, where a stick-thin teenage girl with jut-out cheekbones and shaded eye sockets is more whole and less obvious than a not-quite middle aged woman walking with a dragon's head stick. The girl knows the pecking order here. She is not too shy to look.

People the stick-bearer's own age glance and take care. Their looks contain curiosity too. She should not be here perhaps. She does not have a small child on her arm, a whining teen at her back. Why has this woman come to this foyer alone, for whom is she waiting in obvious pain? Parents drag their careless toddlers back from her wake, pull away little arms and stumpy legs that travel on with no regard, heads turned this way and that, eyes darting distracted from colour to sound and which cannot see that which is directly in front of them. There are assumptions of car crashes and birth defects, cancerous disease and minor ailments. Perhaps this evening out is a last treat. Though the woman appears to have all her own hair – short hair but surely her own. She is not especially grey or wasted, fails to conform to the televisual anti-glamour picture of terminal illness. Maybe then, it is a simple breakage, something that will heal with time. Perhaps the stick she holds is the result of a night out and a fall into the gutter of drunken excess. But there is no certainty. And as long as the reason for the stick is unknown, the there-but-for-the-grace-of-God-ers are forced to offer her the benefit of the doubt. Yes, maybe the woman did cause this injury to herself. But then again, perhaps she was run over in a horrific hit-and-run accident, losing all her babies and possibility in one fell swoop. Perhaps she is dying slowly and painfully of one of the many degenerative diseases that acronym-swamp our present passing. Perhaps this is the last ballet for one who once danced herself. There are so many possibilities and the stick which offers up each one, confirms none. That being the case, the limping, leaning woman is given a wide berth and safe passage through the thronging crowd. A crowd that opens up to let her pass and then, when she has moved from immediate eye-contact space, turns to look after her, watch her go. They hold their breath and wait. She is ill somehow, they would rather she would go.

She can feel them look after her, knows the sensation, though she has usually been the starer not the stared at. Her grandmother had a stick. The old woman who, in her excessive age, rarely left her dark-furnished room except to shout at the little girl when she was playing the tuneless piano too loudly. The piano was for dance, not music. It was not there for itself, what it alone had to offer, it was an adjunct. Without feet and tempo and time steps the piano might as well be silent. The piano should be silent. At night the woman would climb up, high bedstead, candlewick bedspread, placing her stick carefully by the bedside table, it's carved marble head leaning against her glass of water, her headache pills, her stomach pills, her back pills. The black head of a trusty Labrador pinned firmly into a rich maple branch, honed and sanded but with three intentional kinks left in to show its true origins, the Labrador's ears and sensitive snout worn silky smooth by her years of use. This cantankerous grandmother did not have her stick because she was an old woman. To the little girl it seemed astonishing possibility, but she was not always an old woman. Sometimes it came in handy, now that the stairs were sometimes too much, when her rheumatic knee claimed attention, but she'd had this stick since she was just twenty-eight. Fit and healthy then in every way. Though she no longer uses it for its original purpose, she always used a stick for her work.

A dance teacher, she began with a cane and worked her way through several more before this model, old even then, was presented to her as a parting gift from a high-flying student. It is the stick that has pushed in a thousand backsides, turned out a million toes, beaten scores of repeated time steps into the dance hall floor. *Glissade, jeté, pas de chat, tournée, glissade, pas de bourrée*, but no, stop, not like that, and no! The piano stops, the weekday needle is dragged from the gramophone, the Saturday morning pianist reaches for her knitting, the class of girls pause, mid-step, breathless and flushed, sweaty streaks of hair sneaking from heavy-pinned buns. All wrong, you are all wrong! Turn out and right out and here and easy and hold and now – prepare and face and point. But not like that, not like that – like this girls, how many times must I show you? Do it like this. Like me. Like this. Watch me. And then the moment they wait for in every class comes and she lifts her long skirt so all the girls can see the suspenders and corset she wears, firming and framing her body into the straight sylph she was at nineteen when she too flew high and away only to land back home with a bump and the necessity of a small town teaching career. But they did not know that then. They only saw an older woman and her high stockings, ageing legs, veined thighs, the belly-button giggles catching them before the stick did.

Staying too-long weekends with her unwilling grandmother, the stick was the last thing the little girl saw when the old woman turned out the light and closed the box room door behind her, the first thing she heard in the morning when it began its nose-tap tap on the wall next door, its owner crying out for her cup of tea, the in-bed treat she claimed should be also be a treat for the grandchild. A treat to take care of her elderly relative, a privilege to be given the responsibility of the heavy black kettle, the gas fire, the porcelain cup and saucer, the heavy milk with cream floating in yellow globules across the surface of the jug. An honour then, to walk into that dark room where the curtains were never opened and the ivy had been allowed to grow over the French windows and the calendar stayed on the wall, the same faded picture of Our Lady of Lourdes and the exact date it had shown fifteen years ago when the old woman's husband died and the stick ceased its incessant poking at the recalcitrant turn-out of young girls, became instead the only thing left to lean on.

It was not a treat. It was a fearful journey every morning, wracked with the possibility of dead grandmothers and the looming photograph of the long-dead grandfather and the smell of denture fixative and the likelihood of spilt milk to sob over, stewed tea and cracked china. It was never a treat. But today's ballet is. Both for this younger woman and her partner. And so, despite the pain and the looks and with the help of the dragon's head stick, they will go out. Brave the crowds and the braying ballerina children, little girls in itchy princess dresses and pointy plastic tiaras, parents dressing up their dolls to remake the unfulfilling treats of their own childhood. Knowing it cannot work but trying anyway. Impossible to recreate the perfect turn-out but trying anyway.

Her partner taking too long in parking, she makes her way to the disabled toilet, pushing her stick out and across her body as she so often watched the grandmother do. The door is locked, a red engaged sign in a shiny new bolt. This place has recently received lottery funds, the money spent on toilet doors was surely a vital component of the budget application. She waits a minute, another five, the door opens, a mother and toddler walk out. The mother looks at her and before the face, the clothes, the woman before her, she immediately sees the stick. The stick glows in the dim corridor with a sense of entitlement and – in this queue only – privilege. The mother looks down at the toddler as if in explanation, excuse that will turn into defiance if necessary. The stick-bearer doesn't care in the least. But the mother does. And hurries her daughter away.

Finally a lift and several carefully negotiated steps later, she sits beside her partner in a specially arranged aisle seat and waits for the slow confection of the staged picture to begin. The stick-bearer has been far more ill than this. This is a minor physical disability. The burning ache, the throbbing waves are debilitating yes, but minor in that they will pass. Already in the past fortnight the extremes of pain have started to recede. She has been far more ill than this, with no hope of let-up or stick to clear her way. She has stood several times on the edge of insanity, her nails ripping from their tucked-up finger-beds as she tries to claw herself out of the falling pit. And she has fallen and stayed fallen and hidden in the dark and lost in the maze. But then she looked well enough on the outside. She is not one who shows her distress in weight loss or gain, tired eyes or red nose. And she did not have a stick. There was nothing physically wrong with her and no accommodation was ever made for the fact that from her more usual place of pain, this aisle seat would have been a torture, simply walking through that crowded foyer would have taken reserves of courage and fortitude impossible to measure. And even so, because the world demanded it, she has made those walks and sat in those seats and dug her nails deep into her thighs to stop herself from crying out when the hurting was so severe as to undo even the clamped-shut mouth. But those times there was no wand to wave the people around her into semi-fearful compliance. And just as she knows that this physical disability will pass, so too will the other return, the progression and pain inevitable. Knowing this, she has chosen to enjoy her outing with the stick, take advantage of the stature and space it offers, thrill to the helpful feet and pitying glances. There will be time enough for ignorance later.

The curtains part, her partner sits attentive and eager, the stage rises to the applause and a long-dead grandmother adjusts imperfect feet with a heavy stick. At home that evening the lovers dance sugar on to sour plums and remember there will be better nights. Just as there will certainly be worse.

SILK LOVERS

WE HAVEN'T SEEN each other for over two years but we know what to do. We remember the rules. The promise. The vows of silk.

She has prepared herself for this moment. She wears a red silk camisole covered by lush black velvet and topped with sharp red lipstick. Her hair is long and newly dyed dark and covers the nape of her cool neck. She has readied both her own body and the room for his arrival. She has waited twenty-six months for him, she will not spoil this moment by even the most delicate scent of imperfection. There are red rose petals poured before the fireplace. The flames burn high and the petals will be dry before the night is over. The glasses of soft red wine are ready, there is a tiny table holding fingernail size savouries and miniature cream chocolates.

When he arrives, he too is beautiful. Still too beautiful. Still more beautiful than her. He laughs, knowing how hard she has tried, knowing how easy it is for him. He has thrown himself together and, as always, his easy charm discomforts her. He has packed a small bag with all the tools they will need. The tools have not been used for over two years. Still, they are pristine and perfect. As he is.

A sip of wine, refuses chocolate, refuses food and then he is ready. She has no problem following his commands, they flow back like a catechism. He puts the handcuffs on her. They are made of thin paper, almost tissue but even more thin. And smooth.

'Don't rip them, now.' he whispers.

She is led to the chair, her hands cuffed in her lap. Nearly naked.

I continued with the plan even though there was so much else to occupy my time. Watching you. Watching you with her. Watching you watching her. How could you forget to watch me?

She is so careful not to move, not to rip the tiny fibre threads that hold her hands together. The paper immobilises her more effectively than steel. It catches her breath as well as her skin. He places on the blindfold. It is made of thin silk, a single layer and white. Thin enough for her to see through.

She has seen through his deceit too. Though only after he showed it to her. Then it became transparent. She had not known where to look at first.

He undresses himself, to one side, where through the white silk his burnished bronze body is milk chocolate matt brown. He places scissors close by and stands the paper-cuffed woman in front of him. He takes the threads of silk – real silkworm silk they have been saving for this time – and slowly winds the threads between them. His feet to hers. Her legs to his. Their thighs to each other. There were thousands of tiny worms died for this union. Each one softly ripped from its silk and re-laid in a fake cocoon of cotton wool so they could plait themselves together, solder their union.

I left the worms making their silk. I knew we would need it. Eventually.

She receives his body, silk of their skin wound round in silk. This is a winding not a wounding. Not yet. Two smooth bodies stretch, one up, one down to create face-to-face Siamese, twinning themselves in fire-lit melting. Paul hands her the scissors which she holds in her softly cuffed hands. Her arms in front of him and in front of her, her bare arms and the stainless steel against the small swelling of her stomach. The tiny flesh swelling that warms and covers those eggs, holds safe her generations to come.

This shroud is softer even than the skin shroud I have lived in for two years.

There comes a point where the bodies are joined, his arms against her torso, their chests together. His free arms work above and behind her and now they wind their heads together, faces cheek to cheek. She sways, dizzy with looking into his eyes and breathing his breath and is gravity held by his stronger passion.

He always said his was the stronger passion. Not a stronger skin though, I think.

This is not a thought I say out loud.

Now she and he are one, his arms free for a moment until he digs his thumbs, fingers, hands into and under the threads across her back. He is tied to her. She who is returned to him so they can do this thing. This thing they are committed to. This thing that will set him free of her longing, needing. Her disappointment. They spin. Twisting, four feet too close for purchase, rotating on the axis of what they have promised to do, what they bred the worms for, what she has promised to do.

– *Yes, I will. If you ever leave me, I will kill myself.*

– *Promise?*

– I promise.

– Good girl. Now go to sleep.

Difficult to move her hands, thin tissue cuffed inside the tiny convex opening of their two stomachs, so gently to lift one hand above the other where the mingled running sweat has melted her paper bonds. She holds the criss-crossing steel blades and in the moment they fall, in the moment he goes, in the moment the steel meets the narrow resistance of skin and a then little sinew she finds herself worrying about the stain on the silk. The steel travels further in and catches – on an organ. Stomach? Spleen? A lung? She is not clear about the location of these secret parts. Both of them hear a small hiss but they do not know if it is his or hers. A hiss of escaping breath or hiss of escaping venom. They always were too close.

And she need not have bothered about the stains. She caught his blood herself. More full of blood than usual but not especially unpleasant.

When he left me I told him he really shouldn't.

His eyes were very near and she could see he was surprised. It was a look of horror and terror and sex and fucking and then bliss and then – nothing.

He was surprised by the steel, she was surprised by the nothing. She had expected more. Peace perhaps. Or a transcendental awareness. But no, he gave her nothing.

Typical.

She took the silk to a weaver and then to a dressmaker. The dressmaker made a thin band of cloth. Mary kept it. It would have made a lovely blindfold but that the red stains dried ochre and she could no longer see through it.

And there is no point in a blindfold that actually blinds.
You might as well close your eyes.
He did.

FACE VALUE

IT WAS NEVER about me.

It's not about me.

I used to say that all the time, at first when the fuss happened, when it took me from promising to promised, from potential to arrived, when everyone wanted to know who I was and where I'd come from, I said it as my stock answer.

It's not about me.

Because it was true, it wasn't.

Later, in interviews, quite possibly hundreds of interviews at the time of the retrospective, the same old questions, all over again, I said the same, all over again. Or at those stupid parties where I was only in attendance to promote my career, to assist my agent, to do the right thing by the person they'd decided I was, at the events there was always some oily man who'd think it was flattering to contradict my stock answer, to correct me, with an 'Oh but come on, surely you can admit it now . . .'

I'm admitting it now.

It was not about me.

They'd ask too, sitting around the dinner table with friends, this workmate of that gym-buddy, this father of that child at school. I noticed, when I was younger, as a non-mother, that the school gate friends of my friends were the worst. They had nothing to talk about but their children, and even the most besotted parent runs out of child-praise eventually. Halfway through the second bottle, house prices, the government, and the cost of the child-minder covered, the increasingly desperate conversation would finally turn to me.

You don't have children?

What do you do?

And then—

Oh. You're her. You did that piece.

For God's sake. I did about four dozen others, each one of them massively successful, along with a hundred or more less well known, and another couple of hundred that never saw the light of day beyond my studio. But yes, I made that piece. And no, it's not about me.

Maybe I wouldn't mind if they were also interested in the rest of it, the paintings and the tapestries I worked on next, the miniatures I've been making for over a decade now, even the films, self-revelatory as they are. The films are about me, intentionally, deliberately, they are self-sacrificing, self-offering, in a way that nothing else I have made has been. Which might explain why they've not been as successful. Something about the giving up of self, too readily, that doesn't sit right with the viewer. The viewer wants to feel they have prised us from our shell, found the pearl hidden in the gritty oyster. When I offered my pearls, strand by strand, reel by reel (it was film, not video, for some things I am a purist), there was – oddly – less engagement for the viewer. Well, there it is. I have had to accept that not all of my work is received in the same spirit it is offered. I took a while to learn, but I know it now.

I hasten to add, it's not at all that I dislike talking about my work. I'm happy to do so, just not that piece. And because I've been so open about it, because I've said time and again in interviews, that I will talk about anything but that, because I have not lied, not once, when I have discussed my feelings, my lack of feelings, my choice never to speak of it – that is, inevitably, what it always comes back to. The one journalist, interviewer, fan, who is sure that they will force me to reveal all. How it made my career and then broke me. How I went a little crazy for half a year or so after that exhibition. How it changed my life.

I did not change my life. It wasn't about me.

I have been an artist for just over fifty years. I have a well-respected, widely-sold, widely-collected back catalogue. I am known, wanted. Yet of all the work I've ever made, it's always that bloody piece that they come back to – and they will insist on asking about it, all of them. All of you. And so, because it is the truth, and because I know I can never get you to shut up and leave me alone if I just refuse to answer at all, I generally say something like;

But what no-one ever understood, is that it wasn't about me

Then there they are, the almost-winks, the smug insinuations, the little knowing grin that what I'm really revealing is how false we artists are, how blind to our own truths. I am offered the smile that suggests, no matter how honest an artist endeavours to be, that we are never fully revealed in mere words, that we show so much more in our self-deluded hiding than we do in the truths we try to speak.

In short, they – you – do not believe that I do not want to

talk about it. They – you – do not believe that they don't understand the piece and never have done.

I'm telling you now, once and for all, it was never about me.

This is why.

She was nineteen when we met, I was twenty-five. Now, at sixty-four, that six year gap between nineteen and twenty-four seems nothing, but come on, don't you remember how adult you felt at nineteen? And then how, by our mid-twenties, nineteen – all the teens – seemed an age away, the love earned and lost, the passion experienced, the agonising, ecstatic *growing up* that had gone before, that had changed our DNA.

So, she was nineteen and I was her senior by every bit of six years. She was being paid very little by my agent to come over and help me out – my agent's phrase, not mine. My agent's idea, not mine. I've always guarded my privacy, even back then I didn't want anyone in the studio, couldn't bear the idea of someone watching as I worked. I have always wanted a clean line between process and product. The market didn't like the separation then, and they like it even less now, when artist and art-work have become so inextricably linked that buyers believe they are getting a piece of you when they hang you on the wall, when they make space in the foyer, when they build a room just for the work.

Oh yes they did. They created a room just for the work, my work. Astonishing. I was twenty-five – dear God I was young, and I was good. Young and good, there is no more potent combination. True, money is handy, money is useful, but when you're young and talented, money is a sideline. It's only with age that we come to understand its true worth. Someone –

someone malleable, amenable, needy (someone my agent could pay, my agent being old enough to understand the true value of money) – came up with the astonishing idea of creating a room for my work. It took a little persuasion, or maybe a lot, I wasn't involved in the negotiations then, I don't involve myself in them now. Process/product. Keep them apart. In the end, the gallery owners, in collaboration with a middle-aged architect keen to show he wasn't yet past it, decided to use the occasion of my first major exhibition to extend the gallery. Yes, it may have been an idea that was pending, my work may have been just the excuse they needed to demand their Board agree to a bigger spend, or perhaps the architect paid, and certainly my agent fucked. Whatever happened behind the scenes, the effect was that they made a new space specifically for, informed by, my first ever exhibition. They changed a building for me.

They took out two walls, lifted the ceiling, opened a room that had been all about artificial light, proud of the artifice of its light, and made it about the day and the night, and the difference between the two. My work in daylight, sunlight, rainlight, from five until nine – this was a summer exhibition, we considered autumn but dead leaves turn to mulch, and no-one wants chill winds at an opening. The people we wanted to come, to buy, were all about showing themselves, we couldn't be handing out scarves as they entered the building, so summer it was. And there was also my work in sodium yellow – we kept the space open twenty-four hours a day. I know it happens all the time now, but not back then, forty years ago you understand, we were new, brand new. We were a happening for the rich and comfortable. They so wanted to be happening, they just didn't want to have to wear batik. Neither did I.

With the exhibition running twenty-four hours a day, I practically moved in. I needed to, in many ways the exhibition had me as the centre-piece.

It wasn't about me.

When I say they removed a wall, I mean a wall, the entire back wall of an otherwise ordinary 1960s space, and replaced it with steels and raised glass balconies. One end of the room entirely open to the elements. And even though we'd chosen the season to allow for weather, it was an elemental summer, wind, rain, hail, and a solid week of stifling heat. Astonishing. Of course, at twenty-five I thought I deserved it. I thought it was all for love of my work. It was many years before it occurred to me to consider who my agent had had to pay, to fuck, to make my break. And longer still before he agreed to tell me. (You don't want to know.)

Meteoric rise to glory, the bright star from nowhere, art world's hottest new thing. And my poor agent half-broken by the actual, physical, fuckable price he'd had to pay to get me started. I've been paying him ever since. Fifty percent. There's always a ferryman who demands a silvered palm.

I had been working for ten years by the time of that exhibition. Taking my work seriously for ten years. Yes, I did start young, so do many artists. Unlike most of them, I made sure to trash my youthful work, my pathetic teenage experiments, whenever I found a better way, a more successful method. There was no path to be followed through my attempts, no archive to trawl and say see, she went from this to that, here to there, and finally made her way to now. Even then, on the brink of my first exhibition, there was simply a collection of finished work, each piece complete and whole in itself, every one a work of art. And today there is not a single drawing, sketch, first mould, half-cast, Polaroid in my archive.

(Ok, there is, one, a Polaroid, I'm getting to that. It's not about me.)

So. The exhibition was a few months away, they were halfway through tearing down the wall, I was getting daily reports from my agent about how it was looking, how it was going to look. He thought they were pep talks, would gee me up to get on and make, to provide the matter to fill the space, to be the Artist. In reality he was screwing me up. Totally. Terrifying me that they'd actually gone along with the absurd idea, were spending so much time and money and effort on making a space for my work (not for me, it's not about me), and it was all making me a bit crazy. Crazy worried, crazy nervous, crazy upset. They knew the work I'd done to date, there was already a draft catalogue of the pieces I had to show, the work, that was what they wanted, they were all excited and my agent didn't understand why I wasn't thrilled. But it wasn't what I wanted. Not yet. There was something missing, something extra, the thing that would make it fly. And I'd been gnawing away at this lack of the one thing.

I didn't believe in me in the same way my agent did, not yet, not back then. I understood that he saw promise, I understood this exhibition was not to be that of a finished artist, but of one at the peak of her beginning, ready to soar. I understood this, and still I wanted that one thing, the piece that would tip it over into glory. Tip me over. I was exhausted, stressed, I was upset and sobbing on the phone to my agent every half hour – in the time before mobile phones, you understand, when the telephone was a shrill interruption held in place by wires and cables, not a welcome distraction from a dozen other screens.

And so, no doubt to get me off his back, he came up with the brilliant idea of getting an assistant for me. Someone to help with the basic things. Basic things like getting me out of bed before three in the afternoon, basic things like getting me into bed in the first place. Basic things like stopping me destroying all the pieces that had already been assigned places in the exhibition catalogue. In a fit of insomniac insanity, I'd decided they were shit, I was shit, and this exhibition was going to show the whole world my true, talent-free nature.

I may have been twenty-five, but I had the amateur-dramatics of a teenager.

And so she arrived. The assistant-nanny-saviour. The one who was to make all the difference.

Didn't she just.

She was, how shall I put this? Oh yes, perfect. No really, she was. And I don't mean in a Mary Poppins kind of way. She wasn't there to look after me, not really. Nor was she an *All About Eve* kind of assistant. There was no hidden agenda, no – as my mother would have it – 'side' to her at all. She was just perfect. She had a way of making me feel that I could do anything. She behaved as if it was the most natural thing in the world for my work to be getting this attention, that it made absolute sense that the whole open-to-the-elements thing was going on – and this despite the rumours of how much it was costing and that the gallery owners were kicking themselves for agreeing to my agent's absurd demands, conveniently forgetting they'd wanted the renovations, as we always do when confronted by the dust, the brick, the gaping hole in the roof. She made me feel good about it all. She – I can't go on she-ing her, can I? Very tedious for you. So, the assistant, let's call her Lileth. I never use her real name, not now. She didn't like it anyway, her real name, said she'd only used it half a dozen times since she was twelve, had picked a new name every few months and demanded her family try it out. So she might as well have been called Lileth, might as well be now.

Lileth was a god-send. She simply made everything better.

And I loved her for it.

Not in love, I am not gay, not that I've discovered anyway. I'm not really anything much, never have been, I don't have the energy for other people, not when my work demands so much of me. I know I sound like a cliché, can't be helped, it's true. I have tried relationships and I have always been found wanting in them. I cannot give enough because I would rather be in my studio. I cannot agree to be at a dinner at a certain time because I would rather be working. I cannot agree to be with you in bed because, if you help prise me from my work and lift me away from the matter in hand, the in-bed in hand, then there is every chance that finally unfettered from the mundane, I will begin to dream another piece of work. It is only when I am away from the work in hand that I can begin on the work in my head.

Well. Lileth.

Lileth fixed it. She turned my fear into courage, my worry into work. Instead of placating me, Lileth cajoled and spurred me on. Where others told me to sleep, she would say,

Fuck sleep. Get on with it. Who knows when you're going to die? Keep working.

She would bring me food and coffee and wine and a little coke, just a little coke, to keep me up, keep me on it.

Work bitch work.

Our little joke.

Eat bitch eat. Drink bitch drink. Die bitch die.

Lileth was astonishing. She was just right. And the exhibition, when it finally came, when the gallery delays and building permits and problem after problem had been overcome, when that day, that night, that incredible night finally came, it too was astonishing. It too was just right.

But I'm getting ahead of myself. Even with Lileth on my side, there was still the problem of that piece. The one that would make it fly, the one that would hold it all together and also alarm, shock, slap, that would emerge from the whole and be the whole. That piece. The one I was dreaming, looking for, digging into my guts to find and not . . . quite . . . getting it.

And then, I got it. I totally got it, I so got it, I was there when it was got, by me, getting it.

I know, you don't expect ladies of sixty-something in your stories to talk about 'getting it'. That's because you have us in the realm of the grey, where 'old folks' perpetually sing It's a Long Way to Tipperary and talk about the war. Fuck off. I was born in the fifties. I've taken more recreational drugs – and never pretended I didn't like them or they 'did nothing for me' – shagged more men, and I have delighted more strangers, than you've had hot dinners.

I do not bother with hot dinners. Hot dinners are the enemy of the waistline.

I got it. The idea, that idea, the one all the pictures are of, the photographs. The idea that has been used for other people's art, for their photo-shoots, their shop windows, their art-house films and once, God help me, for that bloody awful play where they made all the ushers dress like me.

We made the waitresses dress like me.

It wasn't about me.

Yes, yes, I know you're so cool you have no idea what I'm talking about, do you? You are too young or too uninterested in art, or too . . . God knows, net-savvy. Very well, let me sketch you a picture. Trust me, I'm an artist.

You approach the venue. You know you are approaching the venue because since you turned the corner you have seen me. Every second person you have seen is dressed like, made up to look like, looks like me. At this time in my life and in yours, you have no idea what I look like, but here they are, these young women each one 5'5" tall, each one weighing 110-112lbs and not an ounce more, each one in a long black wig, a deep red dress, absurdly long eyelashes, painted-on eyebrows, and where everyone at the time was wearing nude, nearly-nude, some insipid shade of hippy harmony on their lips, each of these girls wore a gash of dress-matching red. They were barefoot and their toes and fingernails matched, blue. There were black girls, white girls, brown girls, asian girls, oriental. And a few boys who looked like girls. Daring.

And I was one of them.

I was dressed up, made up, designed-up, covered-up to look exactly like all of the girls. The girls who directed you to the entrance, who offered you a drink, who handed you the catalogue, who scuttled back and forth along the street, up the stairs, to the walls where they placed those lovely, lovely red dots. I looked just like one of them.

See? Told you it was not about me.

And in the space itself, the space that we finally allow you into, having left you queuing in the street for a whole half hour, in the space with mannequins dressed like us flying above, with versions of me sitting high in the trees in the garden in the outside that was inside, in the centre of the room, there she lay. Lileth as me, in the glass coffin, the formaldehyde-filled coffin. The woman who was me who was dead who was living. Who was not me. See? It's not about me.

(No I don't think either Tilda or Damian 'improved' on my work. No I do not.)

It was magic, of course. Something to do with mirrors and a very very thin pipe that kept oxygen flowing into her nose and mouth. She was bloody good though, you had to stand very close and watch for some time to see the slightest flicker of an eyelash or a raise of her chest. Almost there, not there. And most people didn't bother to look. They saw the mannequins above, the models in the street, the versions of me/not me climbing the trees outside, looking down at us from the all the windows overlooking that now-open back lot. It was a wonderful idea. And it really worked.

They thought I was terribly clever.

They still didn't know what I looked like.

I was dressed up too, of course.

And then.

My agent stands on a chair to make a speech. He is a small man, and – in the manner of small men – fastidious, fussy, absurdly picky about personal hygiene – which is what, I think, was so painful for him, the things he was asked to do, the things he did, for me, to get me there. Here. I am here and so is he. We have a signal. I hope she sees it, we have rehearsed this, but never with so many people around, we could never have got away with the secret if there were so many people around.

He stands on a chair to make a speech. He begins and I zone out. I have heard the speech, Lileth wrote the speech, they both rehearsed him in it, I am nervous and so I zone out until my cue. Here it is, here it comes,

The absurdly talented . . .

And as I begin to walk towards him, as the room begins to make way for me, as I reach my hand up to the wig to reveal I am she, the one they have been looking for, that of all these women (and some men) it is me who has made all this, up steps Lileth.

Out of the glass coffin. Out of the formaldehyde (not really, we found something that had the same viscosity, the smell).

And now there are two of me.

Wet me and dry me.

And now the waitresses and the assistants and the mannequins – who were never fake, never plastic, who have been harnessed there on wires for hours the poor things – now we all reach up a hand to pull off the wig and then.

Lileth walks to me and I walk to her.

And I pull the wig from her head, I rip the dress from her shoulders, I use the dress as a cloth to wipe the gash of lipstick from her face and Lileth is me.

Naked. Shown. Exposed. Exhibited.

She turns and does the same to me and there we are. Identical down to the tattoo above our left breasts. A half heart each. Same, not mirror, that would have told a different story.

And that was it. The room erupted as you might expect,

as you have been led to expect by every cynical, copycat show that has since copycatted ours. We were the first copies. I was handed a lovely silver gown, Lileth was escorted off to wash and dress, the evening continued.

And someone wanted to buy the girl in the coffin.

And someone bought the girl in the coffin. He signed a cheque there and then, the figure made up by my agent, made up by him on the spot because he didn't think he could get away with it and has been kicking himself ever since, since he's worked out he could probably have asked for double, treble, since the piece has sold and sold and sold. Every time it is sold on to the next proud and hungry collector, I get a little more fame, and all the others of my pieces go up in value. It helps with the few I kept back for me, the one or two I gave him. But neither of us get a percentage of the original, copy-right. And we were all in on the joke, the whole room in on the joke.

(Not Lileth, she was off showering, washing the stink of the heavy water from her skin, breathing deep. Drying her hair, putting on a nice frock, her own makeup, readying herself for her big entrance, her re-entrance, the entrance where they wouldn't notice her at all.)

they didn't notice her at all.

so no-one knew what she looked like really

and she was young

and she didn't quite fit in

and she didn't know how to be with those people

It wasn't too hard to give her one drink and another and another. It wasn't too hard to make sure one of those drinks was laden with a dose that would knock her out, lock her out of herself.

And it wasn't hard . . .

Yes. It was actually. I liked Lileth. I really liked her.

But we had made a deal. Not the buyer and me, the agent and me. We had this idea and we made this deal. I wanted it to be astonishing, I wanted it to fly. I didn't need everyone who came to the exhibition to see how truly astonishing it was, underneath, in reality. I just needed to know that for myself. I needed to know I was making a difference.

Don't all artists want that? To make a difference? To put their stamp on eternity. And what greater stamp is there than to stop another?

Yes, there was a Polaroid. It is of that moment. I do not gloat in it, revel that it was taken, he and I took it together. What do you call them now? A selfie? There is a selfie of he and I holding Lileth. We are holding her on the table as her blood drains out.

My agent was a taxidermist once. In another life. He is not a young men now and even then, he was already middle-aged, had done so much. Lived many lives. In one of them he was a soldier in a far-away country. In another, he was a taxidermist. And in this one, here, he was my agent. And he knew, even before I knew, what I wanted.

In the moment of passing, the point where the blood went from just enough, to just not enough, we were posed. Ready. He clicked the switch.

I have never been very successful with photographs. People like my installations better, my sculptures. They have said, unkind critics have said, that my photographs are a little flat, as if the life is just a little less in them. They may be right.

We took a Polaroid of the one Polaroid, and then another,

and then we had one each. Me, him, and Lileth. He had one to keep as evidence against me, I as one against him. The third sits in the small of her back, beneath the waistband of the red dress, perfectly preserved. As she is.

You'd be surprised how long a punter is prepared to wait for their merchandise, once they know they have it, once they have been on all the art pages as having it, he waited a good three months before we were ready to deliver his goods.

She is great art. She is so life-like they say.

No, she really isn't.

She explains our mortality to us they say.

Well, she explains her own.

She is you and me.

No. She is herself. She is nothing like me. Though we made her up like me, the wig, the dress, the makeup. We made her up like the made-up me.

And she floats in his gallery. You can pay to see her. He does not allow free visitors. He keeps the light a little low. Too low. And sadly, so sadly, there are no windows, no wind or rain. She floats in no water and she reminds me, when I think of her, of a time and a place. That is all. A time and a place where I had one astonishing, audacious idea.

And I executed that idea.

I forget her name. I worked hard to forget her name. I call her Lileth. It suits her.

That collector, the one who is as famous for collecting her as he is for anything else, he has never understood what he paid for, what his zeros bought him. He speaks about her with a pomposity that is almost shocking in its stupidity. About the symbol she is, about the hope she gives him, hope of a form of life after death, hope that humanity can one day understand itself through the image of itself. Art-school bollocks. She is a dead woman in a box of liquid. I gave him hope. (And no, there is no life after death. There is just death. Look at her.)

Although the money was useful, the fame, the notoriety probably made more difference. And anyway, we did not do this to make money, my agent and I. We did it because we could. Because it would be art, real art, living art.

We did it for art's sake.

I called it Me/Not Me.

It was never about me.

COME AWAY WITH ME

CAROLINE COMES HOME to a quiet and empty house. This is no surprise, Pete has been working late most nights for the past month, he's on a tight deadline, his own boss, and in this economy any work is good work. When Pete started out film editors were special, those with his broad training rare, now any kid with a Mac and half a brain can call themselves an editor – and frequently do. Pete is that rare thing, old-school trained, old-school work ethic. This current job is taking much longer than he'd planned, longer than he quoted for as well. But he gets on fine with the director, and he says the project will be astonishing when it's done. That's all he says, Pete firmly believes that the director is the author of the piece, his job is to help the director bring the dream they once held in their mind to reality through the mess of rushes and re-takes. He never talks to Caroline about the work until after she's seen the final edit. He never talks to anyone but the director about it. Not even the writer. Old-school, pecking order, playing the game.

Some nights Pete doesn't come home at all, texts Caroline at ten or eleven or later, when he's finally managed to sneak out for a fag, a fag he promises Caroline he doesn't have, and when he's outside he texts to say he loves her, it's looking like an all-nighter, he'll sleep in the spare room if he comes home, sleep tomorrow if not, kip on the divan in his office if he gets a chance. Pete is twenty-three years older than Caroline, and more thoughtful than any of the young men she knew and loved before she met the one who calls himself her old man. He is not old at fifty-seven, but even Caroline sometimes wonders how it will be when she is fifty-seven and Pete is eighty. She thinks he might be her old man then.

7.35 PM

Caroline opens the fridge. It's been a good day, lots done, lots ticked off on the to-do list. Caroline is a manager for an events company. She doesn't do the running around, the charming and cheering of people, she does the ordering, the sorting, the arranging. Booking taxis and vans, planes and trains, ensuring deliveries get there on time, ensuring people get there on time. She and Pete met when he was editing a corporate video for one of her company's clients. One of those ghastly ra-ra-ra corporate videos, inevitably underscored with Tina Turner belting out 'Simply The Best'. The screening time had been brought forward by a day because the CEO had some emergency he had to attend to in the wilds of middle America and, the client company, terrified that online delivery wasn't secure enough for their ground-breaking yay-us video (underscored with Tina Turner singing 'Simply the Best'), Caroline had offered to go and pick up the edited video herself, take it directly to the conference centre the next morning. Which she duly did, having spent half an hour with Pete laughing at the absurdities of corporate paranoias, then another half hour enjoying a small glass of the single malt Pete always allowed himself on completing a job, and then six hours in Pete's studio, laid out on the divan he kept there for late night naps, laid out for Pete, with Pete, Pete laid out for her.

She opens the fridge for a glass of the cold white left over from yesterday and finds instead a typewritten note, tied to a half bottle of champagne with a thin red ribbon. The note says: Drink Me. Drink Me First. Do Nothing Until You Have Drunk Me. Then Go Upstairs.

Caroline smiles. He remembered. Today is the anniversary of that first night, that night in his studio, that night before the morning when she drove along the M40, exhausted, delighted, smiling and singing to herself, singing 'Simply the Best'.

What Pete has never known is it's also the anniversary of the day she ran out on The Bloke Before a year earlier. Pete's presence that night the perfect antidote to her anniversary-inclined mind.

She takes out a glass, opens the champagne, sits at the kitchen table and drinks it. Does as Pete's asked. She knows he'd expect her to rush upstairs, she usually would, but this is so sweet, such a lovely gesture. She'll drink the fizz and then go to see what's next. What Pete has waiting for her.

The half bottle lasts two and a half glasses, on the half she decides it's time to go up. It's 7.55 pm now and she's slightly fuzzy. Happily fuzzy. Loving her old man, sure no man her own age would have remembered, made such a gesture, known how much she enjoys these games.

She does enjoy games. Pete and Caroline enjoy games.

7.58 PM

Caroline turns on the bedroom light. In the middle of the bed, slightly on Pete's side of the bed actually, is an open suitcase. The small, wheelie suitcase they use when one of them goes away for a night for work. Caroline hates going away for work, Pete even more so, they both try to get out of it whenever they can, but sometimes needs must, and sometimes they have to go. They have been sharing this suitcase for almost five years, it doesn't get a great deal of use.

Sitting in the open suitcase is an A5 envelope, and inside the envelope are tickets and her passport. Caroline's name on first class return tickets to Venice.

There is another note with the tickets, printed in blue this time, it says a car will be there to pick her up at 9 pm. She has an hour to pack, bring clothes for two days, bring clothes for warm days and slightly chilly nights by the water. Bring herself. Bring love. Bring five years of them.

8.55 PM

Caroline has showered and packed. She is ready. She carries the little case downstairs, her handbag already on her shoulder, and a thought occurs to her. It's a wonderful, wonderful gesture, but there is a tiny part of her that thinks it's also a very little bit odd. They have played games before, ever so slightly scary games. Caroline doesn't want this to be a game, she wants it only to be fun. She runs back upstairs, opens the drawers on Pete's side of the their shared chest of drawers. She checks. His passport is gone, good. She looks in the drawers below. She's not sure, but she think some pairs of his boxers are missing, a couple of pairs of socks. The doorbell rings. She opens the wardrobe, his suit is missing, the not-quite-best suit he likes to wear out for a nice dinner. Not that they go out that much, his work, her work, recently they've been thinking it's as nice to stay in for the night as go out. The doorbell rings again and Caroline calls that she is coming. She feels good now. Safe in the knowledge that, if this is a game, it's one he's playing with her. Safe in the knowledge that Pete will be waiting for her, at the airport, in the hotel maybe. Safe.

9.05 PM

Caroline is in the car, the driver knew her name and which airport she is going to – Heathrow, Terminal 2. Lucky, she hadn't checked herself. She wonders if the driver will hand her a package, more instructions, more messages. She texts Pete to tell him he is brilliant, there is no reply but she wasn't really expecting one. She knows Pete likes to maintain the mystery of his games, when he plays games. They are on the M4 and almost at Heathrow before she has stopped wondering where Pete is now, she worries that perhaps she is meant to pay the driver. Pete's not as good as she is with cash, with always making sure she has enough cash. Caroline has just-in-case ten and twenty pound notes tucked in the back of her wallet, in the zipped section of her handbag, in a little plastic purse in her makeup bag. Just in case. So Caroline knows she has enough cash, but she wonders if Pete has paid the driver anyway, she's usually the one to pay the driver. They arrive at Heathrow. Pete has paid.

10 PM

This is the last flight to Venice tonight. There is no queue for First Class and Caroline slips thorough security quickly and easily, is directed to the First Class lounge.

10.45 PM

Boarding is announced and just as she walks the easy distance to the boarding gate a text comes. It is from Pete. 'There will be a water taxi waiting for you. Look out for the sign with your name on it. I love you. Pete.'

A water taxi. Caroline and Pete haven't used the water taxis before, they seem so extravagant, so unnecessary when the journey on the vaporetto is easy and smooth anyway, when that round trip via Murano, past the cemetery is so easy. They have been to Venice three times before now, have stayed in San Marco and Dorsoduro. She wonders if the taxi will take her to one of those hotels or somewhere new. Caroline is tired, and boards the plane, happy to lean back in her seat, to take the meal offered, the wine, to eat and drink and then she sleeps.

APRIL 12TH 1.15 AM, LOCAL TIME

Caroline sleeps most of the flight and wakes groggy, the champagne and the wine has muddied her mind. And she's very tired, it's been a long week, tonight was meant to be Friday night nothing, Saturday sleep in. But her bag is the third off the carousel, and then she is through the green lane and out into arrivals where the nice young man holds a broad card with her name on it. CAROLINE HUNTER. He speaks almost no English and she has even less Italian but they know the international signs of yes that's me, and follow, and please, take your seat, here, in this ludicrously luxurious little speedboat that is also a taxi, all wood panelling and lace curtains. And then they are off, he is driving the boat and Caroline is wide awake, can't keep the grin from her face, they are powering down the channel to the island and she can see the old lights, and the towers, walls and there, just peeking over the wall, a spire, the top of the campanile perhaps, it might be San Marco, it might be another church, it is there and gone as the taxi speeds over the waves thrown by the boats it passes. He is a young man and he drives like a young man.

1.45 AM

The ride, the water, the waves, the wind are successful in their conspiracy to please; Caroline is wide awake and delighted. The taxi enters the Grand Canal, the Guggenheim palazzo is on her left, Caroline remembers when she and Pete went there, how they spent the whole dinner that night talking about what they'd do with a house like that, what it must be like to live in such a place, to have the water so close, so part of your home.

She thinks about the first time she came here, with The Bloke Before, with John. So many mistakes with him and then that last mistake, coming to Venice, agreeing to come away with him when she'd already had enough of his possessiveness, arguing with him and running out of the nasty little bed and breakfast he'd booked for her birthday treat, running out and leaving him. Calling the B&B owners and struggling for the right words, the language to pass on the message that she'd gone back to London, heart-wrenching messages from John begging her to come back, to try again, and then, as the days and weeks wore on, angrier messages, messages she has tried hard to forget. She hadn't gone back, she stayed on in Venice, furious with John for being so demanding and yet calling her possessive. Caroline was certain something had been going on and, sure enough, the next day, watching him across a square she'd seen him chatting with a couple of girls, chatting and then laughing and then yes, just as he'd accused her of the day before, there was the exchange of numbers, then the kiss on both cheeks, too friendly, too lingering. John was the slut he'd called her and she knew he was.

Caroline looked down at her handbag, Pete's notes inside, with her return ticket. God, she was lucky she'd run from John. But that first time here with John, when they'd arrived at the airport and walked down to catch the vaporetto and she'd assumed they were riding the waves to an island. She hadn't quite understood, not from the books or the movies, that it really was all water. No roads, no cars. Caroline had not been able to imagine no cars. And all those bridges, the dead ends, the alleyways that appeared to go somewhere and just returned to water instead.

That was then, with John. Caroline knows better now, knows Venice better. A little at least, she knows it with Pete, where they like to stay, to eat, to drink.

Caroline is not with Pete and this is a lovely gesture on his part, but actually she is starting to feel a little lonely, it is dark and colder than she expected and Pete's surprises, his games, are all very well, but she prefers to play with him rather than

for him. She will explain this, tomorrow perhaps, over breakfast, that she is grateful for his romantic gesture, and maybe,
anyway, it would be more fun to be together than apart, in
touch than not.

San Marco is on the right now, they are closer to the southern shore, so maybe the taxi is turning off soon, the boy-racer
driver has slowed a little, Caroline is sure there must be laws
about driving too fast here, though the canal is wide and virtu-
ally empty. It is late, later than at home. The Academia Bridge
and then an opening, the taxi turns south, he drives her down
one wide canal then into another more narrow, then there are
smaller turns, dizzyingly fast, even though she realises, techni-
cally, they must be driving slower, the boats speed seems faster,
the canal is so narrow here she could reach out and touch the
sides. The tide is out and the taxi is low in the water, the edges
of the canal loom over her, Caroline does not want to touch
the sides. It is dark, cold, wet. She looks ahead and now it
seems as if they must have come back on themselves. If she
leans to the side, if she looks past the young driver's head, she
can see the Doge's Palace, more distant now, it is down one,
two, maybe three widenings of this narrow canal they are now
in. Then under another bridge, very low this time, another left
turn, another left, back in on themselves again and then the
taxi stops. It is dark, and the silence is sudden. He turns and
smiles. Here.

2.20 AM

Here. There is no hotel that she can see, no welcoming light.
There is no light, just the faint milky sheen from a half moon

185

high above night-white cloud. Caroline repeats the boy racer's words as he picks up her bag and jumps up on to the canal side. There is apparently no dock either. Caroline had been envisioning one of the pretty little side-canal docks she'd seen from the Grand Canal, the lovely hotels with their own landings. She takes the boy's hand and he hauls her up on to the waterside. She slips a little, grazes the hand he isn't holding, brings it to her mouth without thinking, partly to stem the yelp she doesn't want to let out, partly the animal desire to lick a wound. She tastes a little grit, unravelled skin, maybe a tiny touch of blood, but the predominant taste is the dark silty water of the lagoon, a flavour of algae too, that particular soft pale green that is the water of Venice on a bright blue day. Pete's ex-wife had those light green eyes, the colour of the water. He told her, once, only once, she didn't want to know and Pete never mentioned Susannah's eyes again. The young man is standing her up straight now, looking into her eyes, she doesn't understand the words, but she knows he is concerned. Caroline is exhausted, she has half-fainted, swooned – has she swooned? She thought women only did that in old romance novels, but then, she is in Venice, Venice is an old romance novel in itself – she stands straight. She is fine, assures the young man in English he, in his turn, does not understand. But the hotel, where is the hotel, she asks. These are words he knows. He smiles, nods, leans down to tie up the boat, a rope procured in semi-darkness from a corner. He takes her bag with one hand and guides Caroline with the other. He holds the hand she has grazed and there is almost a comfort in his skin on her ripped skin, the sting of his own hand's moisture getting into the flesh of her own. One corner, another, and then, just at the point Caroline was going to dig in her heels, say no more, try to call Pete again, call out for anyone, worried, frightened, not wanting to follow this young man, with his warm hand and insistent yes/*si*/yes/follow/*andiamo*, there it is, the Hotel Angelo. Tiny sparkling lights around a door and the windows on either side. A discreet sign and an older man in a dark coat at the door, waiting for her. He thanks the driver and pays him, taking Caroline's bag and ushering her in, welcoming her, expecting her. *Benvenuta Signore Caroline.* He pronounces the 'e'. The man knows her name, her room is ready, come in.

2.30 AM

The man takes her passport, she signs a form, they show her to a room. Pete is not there. Caroline wants to cry. The room is beautiful, a suite not a room, a sitting room opening on to a bedroom opening on to a bathroom, all soft lighting and cool minimalist but warm too, comfortable, balconies from both sitting room and bedroom. There is a locked door, just off the sitting room, an extra bedroom for a family of guests Caroline assumes. It's more a small, elegant apartment than a hotel room, but there is no Pete. Caroline even goes outside on to the balcony, just in case he is hiding. He isn't. She sees the boy racer below, on his phone, talking in quiet, fast Italian, smoking. He unhooks the rope and, without putting down the phone, without taking the cigarette from his mouth, without stopping talking, he sets the boat into gear and drives away. She watches him go, then there is silence. Water, lapping, only just, and silence. Caroline shakes her head. This is insane, she is angry now, Pete's just being stupid. It's no fun without him. She will go in and call him and shout and they will have a row but it doesn't matter, she wants to hear Pete's voice. She wants Pete.

A knock at the door and she runs to answer it, calling his name, believing him on the other side of the door. A young woman stands there smiling, pushing a trolley. There is a huge bunch of flowers, spring flowers, a half bottle of champagne – Caroline shakes her head, half bottle again, a single glass she notes, her anger rising further, and an envelope. She points to the envelope and asks the girl about it, Did he leave this? My boyfriend? But the girl shakes her head, *mi dispiace, non parlo* . . . she pulls out a plate of fruits from the bottom layer of the trolley, bread too, some cheese, and then leaves. *Buona notte.* Caroline doesn't want her to go. She doesn't want to be alone. The girl closes the door behind her and Caroline opens the envelope.

There is a single piece of paper inside, and a small pill, just one, in a foil wrapper. There is no writing on the foil.

The paper is a printed email: Sorry, I meant to be there waiting for you. Impossible delays here. I'm getting the first flight out in the morning. Eat, Drink, Sleep. Sleeping pill if you want. I'll be there by the time you wake up.

Caroline opens the champagne, she eats a chunk of melon. She is close to tears. She tries Pete's phone but it goes to answer. Tries again, leaves a message, trying not to sound angry, needy, Pete hates needy. Hangs up realising she probably sounds both. She is lonely and tired, Caroline is not very good at her own company, not at night. In the day she can happily spend twelve hours at a stretch alone, but once dusk hits she hungers for other people, for noise, interaction, warmth. Pete. She turns on the TV and turns it off again. The middle-night Italian talk show women with their porn-star makeup and brash clothes are not the warmth she wants. Caroline sighs.

She goes to the bathroom, takes off her makeup, checks all the doors and windows are locked, double locked, drops her clothes on the floor and takes the sleeping pill and the half bottle of champagne to bed.

Caroline drinks, swallows, sleeps.

APRIL 12TH, 11.15 AM

Caroline wakes, disoriented, her head is fuzzy from champagne and the sleeping pill and no water, no food. No Pete. She has woken up and he isn't here. Caroline sits and then falls back on to her pillows, these big, soft, white-cottoned pillows that are so ready for her tears. And then Caroline is standing and rushing for the bathroom, dizzy head and stumbling feet, arms out to find walls, doors, knee smashing into bedside cabinet. The blackout blinds kept night light, street light out last night, now they turn the room into a labyrinth, she finds a door, runs a sweaty hand up and down the wall, clicks a switch, light blinding, mouth open, kneeling at the toilet, throwing up. After she has washed her face, cleaned her teeth, Caroline takes the white towelling gown from the hook in the bathroom and walks into the bedroom.

She finds her phone and there are three texts from Pete, all saying the same thing. Sorry. Sorry. Sorry. Each one giving a later departure time. The last text says 6.15 pm arrival. He will be there for dinner. He. Will. Be. There. For. Dinner. Caroline is not sure why Pete is still trying to promise, when clearly he has no power to do so. Caroline knows how angry he must be, how Pete hates delays at the best of times. She wants to text him back, to placate him, to tell him it's fine. And she doesn't want to as well. She wants him to miss her as she is missing him, she wants to cry and shout and stamp her foot and complain. She texts back simply; Don't worry. I love you. See you later.

Caroline is hungry. She has an afternoon in Venice, alone. She will go out, she will eat, she will enjoy herself. There are things she knows she wouldn't do if Pete were here, tourist shops full of pretty little bits of Murano glass Pete would never go into, windows of carnival masks he loathes. Pete hates all that tourist crap. Caroline is sure he's right, and yet a part of her, the part she doesn't dare show Pete, is still attracted to it, to being – more honestly – the tourist she is. She will walk over the Rialto Bridge and go to San Marco and she will order insanely expensive coffee and cake that Pete believes only stupid American tourists would eat and leave the kind of tip Pete never would and look at all those shops that spin off the square. And when she has finished wasting money she will come back to the hotel and get dressed up and she and Pete will have dinner and they will come back to that big fluffy bed and fuck and sleep together and it will all be fine. She can bear being alone in daylight and Pete will be here by night.

12.55 PM

Caroline walks downstairs, there is no-one at reception, no-one to leave her key with, to return her passport, there is no bell either, it is all quiet, cool, the place feels empty. She imagines this is a good time for the staff to take a break, grab a rest between breakfast and checkout and cleaning the rooms and then the after-lunch rush as the morning flights that left London and Paris and Madrid land and the new guests check in. She puts the heavy room key in her bag and leaves the hotel, the door locking behind her.

I PM

Caroline turns right. This is not the way she came in, she makes a note of the street name, and where the door is in relation to the water, to the canal off-shoot where the taxi dropped her. She looks up and can see, past the narrowing perspective of tall buildings on either side of the small street, that the sky is very light-blue, high white cloud filtering the pure blue she remarked on the last time they were in Venice, and the first time in Venice too, that time with John. A city girl, Caroline always looks up to the sky. Not for her the checking of fields or flower beds or hedgerows to judge the weather or the season, it is all in the sky. She likes a high sky, and a lot of it. These narrow streets, narrow canals make her claustrophobic. She heads out of the small street and into a larger one and then another wider still. Across a bridge she finds a footpath leading alongside a canal, into another canal, broader now, and then sees what she is looking for, walks along and up to the Grand Canal. This is how she will find her way around, this is how she will orient herself. She will not get lost. She looks across the water, north-east to the Doge's Palace, to her right the span of the Academia Bridge, she knows the Rialto is all the way round to her left. She will go to the Rialto, because Pete would not. She will cross it and may even buy herself a mask, something that hides her eyes, with feathers perhaps, because Pete would not like it. She will waste money on things only stupid tourists do. Pete isn't here and Caroline is.

2.15 PM

Caroline has eaten ice cream – cherry, rich, syrup dripping from the creamy vanilla ice, fat cherries squirting sweet juice into her mouth when she bites into them. She has stopped for coffee twice, both times an espresso, both times standing at the bar, paying the cheaper price, the price she cannot pay with Pete who likes to sit, take his time to look around. She has stood at the bar and talked to no-one and sipped the bitter coffee made easier with sugar and been glad, almost glad, to be alone.

2.45 PM

Caroline is standing in front of the four horses, the ones from Constantinople they keep here, upstairs in San Marco. She's been here with Pete but he wouldn't let her touch them. He was right, no-one is supposed to touch, there's a sign saying no photos, no touching, and Pete wouldn't let her take their picture either, led her outside to get close to the copies standing above the front doors to the big church. But Caroline has wanted to touch the originals since then, and now she does. She walks around the barrier, ignores the camera she knows is watching, and stands before each horse. There are a few other tourists in here, not many, it's as if no-one really cares about these horses. That's one of the reasons Caroline wants to touch them, she thinks they should be outside, that they shouldn't have to mind about the weather and the pigeons, wants them to be open to the world as they must have once been, long ago, far away. The other tourists are tutting, one uses it as a chance to take a photo, his camera flashes just as Caroline turns her head, a hand reaching out to the fetlock of the first horse, and from the light, from behind the light, blinded by the flashlight, Caroline thinks she sees a face she recognises.

A security guard comes and Caroline is asked in very polite English to leave the building, the man with the camera is asked to leave too. She does as she is told.

2.58 PM

Outside, in the square, the bells about to ring, people gathering to listen, Caroline rubs her eyes, behind her palms, behind her lids, she sees the negative image of the man with the camera that made the flash and also the man standing behind him, watching her, the man she thought she recognised. Caroline doesn't know what John looks like now. The man she thought she saw looked like John might look, now.

Caroline feels sick. The ice cream and the bitter coffees and the adrenaline rush of getting kicked out of the church, it is that, it's definitely that, it can have nothing to do with thinking she saw John behind the man, behind the light of the flash. That would just be paranoid.

3.01 PM

The bells have begun to ring and it's too loud for her here, ears fuzzy with ringing, bile in the back of her throat. Caroline walks across the square, beneath the portico, takes a right down a street, any street, it doesn't matter. She walks for ten minutes, fifteen. The afternoon sun is beginning its descent, light angles into the narrow paths between buildings, the high white clouds of earlier are burned off, and every now and then the sunshine catches a window, bouncing sunlight back into her eyes and each time it's like the flash going off, the man taking the photo and the man behind him, and now Caroline is sure it was John, looking, just looking, not surprised to see her, just there. Looking. Watching.

3.35 PM

The turn she just took has led her down an alleyway between two houses and out to a dead-end. Caroline stops as the alley peters out, falling into water. She can see where it would continue. Over there, across a narrow canal, just wide enough for two small boats to pass each other, over there is a café where people sit and chat, drinking coffee and wine, drinking spritz, the Aperol bitter in the bubbles. They are close enough for her to hear the American accents of the group of young people, talking about where they will go tomorrow, about a friend who will join them later. Two middle-aged women sit side by side, they speak more quietly, but even so, the canal here is so narrow that Caroline thinks she can hear their Italian lady voices, their soft, discreet murmurs in someone else's language.

Both women are beautifully groomed, each with a dog in her lap. The dogs should match the women, they too are beautifully groomed, coiffed hair poking out from little dog-shaped coats on their small, round bodies, but the women look as if they are holding the wrong dogs, each one holding her friend's dog. The street continues past the café, but Caroline cannot walk down it, the water is in the way. To her left, past a row of houses is a bridge, but the houses are right on the water, there is no walkway alongside them. There are two boats moored here at her feet. For other people, for locals, this would not be a dead end at all, this would be an opening, an exit, a way out, a way home. For Caroline there is nothing to do but go back, she begins to turn, looking down the alleyway behind her, into a cooler darkness now, the lower sun can no longer reach down here and the alley looks dark, its distant opening into a broader street hidden in shadow. There is nowhere else to go but back and as she turns Caroline hears a loud laugh from the group of young people on the other side of the water. She doesn't know why, but she feels like they are laughing at her. She twists around, and now she's sure the young woman at the rear of the group, head thrown back in laughter, head leant forward to kiss the young man beside her, kiss him long and hard, Caroline is sure she's the chambermaid who brought the trolley last night, with champagne and food and the sleeping pill, the young woman who spoke no English. But the young woman's face is obscured by the young man she is kissing, and they were all speaking English she is sure, speaking with American accents. Caroline takes a deep breath, she feels tears behind her eyes and she does not want to cry, doesn't want to feel sick, is in danger of doing both. She plunges back into the alleyway, pushes past a Spanish couple who are clearly walking in the wrong direction, who are lost and start to ask her directions, pull out their map, and then they take a closer look at her face, step back, allow her to pass. Caroline rushes on, walking down streets and along narrow canals and across bridges, everywhere other accents, Spanish and French and English and American, is no-one here Italian? She thinks of an Italian friend at home whose family come from Venice, who said no Italians can afford to live there any more. And then she shakes her head again. What is she thinking of her friend for? Why is she thinking of John?

3.25 PM

Caroline stops, she is in a small square, there is a bar at either end, a church in the middle. She goes to the closest bar, sits down, orders a coffee and a glass of prosecco. Her hands are shaking. What is she thinking of? She isn't thinking at all. This is insane. Of course that girl wasn't the same girl from the hotel, there must be hundreds of young girls in Venice, all of them tourists or students or here with boyfriends and girlfriends. All the young girls look the same anyway, Caroline is on the edge of calling herself a woman, not a girl anymore. These days, when she sees a young woman she sees the fine skin, the fresh eyes, sees the new. Sees what Pete saw in her at first and what he maybe sees no longer. Sees what John saw in her. She smiles, the coffee and wine arrive, she takes a long slow sip of both, one after the other. Stop it. Stop it. Her hands slowly stop shaking. John always said she was paranoid, that he was not possessive, as she thought him, just loving, wanting to take care. Pete's the other way, accuses her of jealousy sometimes, he says she has no reason for it, that she's imagining things, imagining flirtations, potential. There must be hundreds of young girls in Venice, thousands. Caroline finishes the prosecco, orders another.

4.10 PM

Her phone beeps. She is low on battery, should have plugged it in last night, wasn't thinking, must start thinking. It's Pete again. About to turn off my phone. Plane taxiing. Air steward has glared at me twice. I love you. Coming.

Caroline smiles, nods to herself, breathes out a breath she didn't even know she had been holding. She rubs her neck, downs the now-cold coffee, orders a third prosecco. She texts back, it doesn't matter that Pete won't get this, it doesn't matter that he will only pick it up when his plane lands, it matters that she tells him. I love you. I'm waiting for you.

4.40 PM

Caroline pays for her drinks, stands, she's actually a little drunk now, enjoying feeling a little drunk now. She should probably eat, will get back to the hotel, find her way through these insane streets and canals. She'll stop on the way and buy something to eat from one of those shops that sell fat-filled breads to tourists hungry from sight-seeing, something with cheese and aubergine and courgette and salami. Antipasti in bread, that's what Pete calls it, disapproving. He likes long Italian meals, each course an adventure in itself, doesn't think the Venetians should accommodate tourist desires, doesn't think of himself as a tourist at all. Caroline probably has three hours before she needs to be ready for Pete, two to be on the safe side, she will make her way back slowly, eat, sober up, wash and dress and be ready for the surprise he has been un-ready for. All will be well.

5 PM

Caroline has found her way back to the Grand Canal, she didn't realise she'd come so far, there are signs for the Ghetto back behind her. She and Pete came here the first time they were in Venice together, it was sad, and lovely, to see the old synagogue, to see where the word came from, and then Pete found an amazing restaurant that night, quite close to the Ghetto and they'd eaten so well, so happily. When they walked out into the night she was amazed it was so late, and so very quiet, so different to other parts of the city, busy un-til late at night. It's quiet here now, too, quieter anyway than back where she thought she'd been heading, to the Rialto. She heads east again, a falling sun behind her, in and out, unable to walk directly alongside the Grand Canal here, she tries to keep the sun behind, even when she has to turn north again. Eventually there are more people, and signs, and a vaporetto stop, and Caroline buys her ticket, boards it, the beginning of a headache coming with sunset. Caroline gets off at San Toma, between the Rialto and Academia, it must be close to the hotel. She wishes she'd thought to bring a map, to ask the man at reception for a map, but she didn't. At home Caroline never gets lost, prides herself on knowing her way round London, even the farthest reaches, or the most winding parts down by Greenwich and Canary Wharf, prides herself on always knowing where the water is. Here she is where the water is, always. Her compass is waterlogged. She will wander and she will find it. She remembers the street name, the canal name, she will find it.

5.10 PM

Caroline has a feeling she is close, she is walking alongside a narrow canal, the footpath here is narrow too. She is behind two men, one older, greyer than the other. They have Australian or New Zealand accents, she can't tell the difference, and they're laughing about a girl they both know. You should have seen her face, one says. Mate, I don't need to see her face, I can see your face! And they laugh and the greyer one slaps the other one on the back and they stop for a moment, one is lighting a cigarette and Caroline needs to get past them, she says excuse me, excuse me, can I get past here? They shuffle to the side, she hears the match strike, the flare of warm light, and Caroline turns to thank the two men. She turns and recognises one of them, the older one, with greying hair, is the man from the hotel's reception, she knows for sure he is from the hotel and she knows this because he sees her, sees her looking and nudges his friend and they both look up. Shit, the older one says. And he turns away, his head to the wall, but it's too late and Caroline wants to throw up again, wants to grab him and ask what the fuck is going on, wants to reach out to the man, but her legs don't want that at all, her legs and her gut are terrified and she runs instead, runs away from them, rushing on to where she thinks the hotel is. Her head doesn't want to go to the hotel, it isn't safe, can't be safe, but her legs and gut propel her, now pushing past a young couple, Caroline shoves them both out of her way. They are English and yell at her in surprise, yell that she should be careful, there's no need for that, what's her problem.

Caroline doesn't know what her problem is. And she does, running on, running slowing, walking now, breath catching, a stitch in her side, walking toward the hotel anyway, sure she knows these streets now, sure she knows where she is. Caroline does know what her problem is. She knows she hasn't been able to believe these messages from Pete, not really, knows Pete would never let her down like this, knows he would have been at the airport, in the hotel, would have been waiting. And now she stops, cold, sick to her stomach and bile rising again in her throat. Because she knows, actually, that Pete doesn't really do surprises, that while they have their games, Pete has never really done surprises, that the real surprise she came home to on Friday evening was that it was so out of character for Pete. So in character for John.

5.40 PM

The sun is still lighting the sky, but it's darker and cooler in the narrow street leading to the hotel.

On the other side of the small canal just here, beneath a shop awning, standing with his back to her, Caroline sees a man texting. She sees the man and she is sure she knows who he is, knows the back of him. The man stops texting, watches his phone's screen. A few seconds later her own phone beeps. A text comes through, from Pete's phone. I'm here. Landed.

Won't be long. Can't wait to see you. It's been way too long.

The man turns, he doesn't see Caroline looking. It's John, Caroline is sure it is John. He looks in through the window of the shop, waves, walks on, away down the little sidewalk alongside the canal, down to a bridge that will bring him back to this side of the canal, where the hotel is.

The hotel has her bag and her things and her passport and Caroline wants nothing more than to run from here, run from this place, but her phone is almost out of battery and the charger is in her room and her stuff is in the room and maybe, maybe she is as paranoid as John always said, maybe she's just exhausted and maybe it will be all right, but whatever it will be she needs to charge her phone and she needs to get her things and so she runs back down the street to the hotel and opens the front door and lets herself in.

5.50 PM

There is no-one in reception, just as there was no-one earlier. She runs upstairs and into the sitting room of the suite, slamming the door behind her, locking it. Caroline looks around. She takes in the room properly, sees that while it is a beautiful room, cool and clean, lovely lines, it is missing some of those things even the finest hotel rooms must have. The sign on the wall about emergency exits. The list by the telephone of charges, useful numbers to call. The explanation in five different languages of how to work the TV and satellite. She remembers there were no signs downstairs either. Nothing on the reception desk that was, after all, just a counter really, a plain counter, with nothing on it, no message about breakfast or check out, no handy pile of maps and leaflets for unprepared tourists. Caroline realises she has seen no other guests. The only people she has seen are the chambermaid and the man behind the desk. And that she did see them when she went out today and they were speaking English, she wasn't mistaken. Caroline has let herself believe. And now she lets herself understand. She walks over to the locked door, it opens. Behind it is a kitchen. A normal, elegant, newly-fitted kitchen. This is not a hotel room. It is an apartment.

Her phone beeps. She doesn't want to look. Can't stop herself looking.

I'm in the bedroom. Waiting.

And even though she doesn't want to go, and even though her gut and legs are trying to hold her back, Caroline overrules them this time and walks herself to the bedroom door.

She opens the door.

Pete is on the bed. And a lot of blood. Pete's blood, on the bed, bloody Pete.

And the phone beeps again and she hears the sitting room door, the door from the corridor, the door she locked, she hears it being unlocked.

And she looks at the phone as the door handle turns and her phone says See? I told you it was a surprise.

And Caroline wants to move, to scream, to run, but nothing is working, her legs, her mouth, nothing is working, nothing can move her, she is stuck staring at Pete, Pete's blood, stuck waiting as the steps come closer behind her

And then a hand is on her shoulder and still her mouth won't open, her voice won't come and John says See? I told you I'd always remember you.

THERE IS AN OLD
LADY WHO LIVES
DOWN OUR STREET

I'M THE OLD lady who lives on your street, the one you smile at, unsure, as you rush for the train.

I'm the old lady who lives on your street, when you look for me in snow, or in rain, I'm gone.

I'm the old lady who lives on your street.

Shall I tell you how I came here? Yes? Good.

Cuddle up, come closer, listen tight.

There is an old lady who lives down your street, and she wasn't always old and she wasn't always me, but she is now. I am now.

I had a house, just like you, and a husband, like you do too, and some children, pretty pretty babies, shining and new. And time passed and he passed away and they passed through, my babies all grown, stopped in, stopped off, dropped off their little ones, but not often, only if they needed my help. And this house, that house, the house we lived in, with rooms so many, so wide, corridors so long – I said to those children, my children, now grown and strong, I suggested, just suggested,

I could sell the house, go away, have a trip, spend some time, some money and time, some of the money that buys time, spend it on me.

And my children who were no longer children took it in, slowly, they can be so slow, and when they understood they were suddenly squabbling toddlers again. Who will feed my babies, who will care for my children, don't you want to be a good granny, kind granny, helpful granny? What about us? Where is our home if you're not in it? Where is our past if you don't hold it? Where are our memories if not in these rooms? What about us? Us? Us?

And behind that, a single, slow, held note at the edge of listening, a note that whined, insistent and high, 'What about, what about, what about our inheritance?'

What about that indeed.

Fair enough, it was a big house, that house, still is, but it's no longer my house.

It was the fifth anniversary of his death. One of the children sent a text, my eldest girl, good like that, always texts me about important things, her father's anniversary, my birthday, Christmas.

The middle one called, in a hurry, just wanted to say, you know, Mum, I mean, today, isn't it? Today? I think?

The baby was away, work, holiday, they sound the same to me, but she sent roses, dark red roses like her dad used to. Sweet. Neither of them ever asked me what flowers I like. I don't like roses.

And the other two, I'm sure they thought of us. It's the thought that counts that counts, right?

It was his anniversary and I took myself out for lunch. Our

place, a restaurant long fallen from fashion. I wore a frock he liked, long fallen from fashion, and when I left the restaurant I was – admit it – yes, I was, tipsy, cheery, merry. Still widowed though.

I could have taken a cab home, that would have been an extravagance. I could have caught the tube, that might have been wise. But I didn't, there was a street before me, a street of lovely shops and fine things and then I was walking down that street, walking like I owned it – I, who never go into those shops, the ones with young men on the door, and elegant ladies inside. But I had dressed well for my singular lunch, and I walked down the street with my head held high.

And then I saw it.

In the window.

A bracelet in white gold, linking emerald green stones, diamond pieces between each one. I assumed it was paste, it was in the window after all, but it was still so lovely, so . . . bright, light, green.

And it called me, called me in to the shop.

I went in.

I asked the young man, I just asked him, that bracelet in the window, how much is it? A shop like that, they wouldn't put the real thing in the window, and I know imitations can be pricey, but even if it's five thousand, maybe I could, maybe I shouldn't, but maybe I could. Five babies, five empty bedrooms, five years alone.

He smiled and said, would you like to try it on?

Yes, thank you, I would.

He brought me a chair. And the security guard came, with a big set of keys, and they opened the window and pulled out the whole display case, locked display case.

They went into the back room and I waited.

They returned and presented me with the bracelet on a cushion of gold silk.

And I held out my arm and he put it on me and my arm, my arm had never looked more beautiful.

I asked him how much and he said half . . . and then stopped, because he knew it sounded too big, too much, ridiculous. I smiled, go on, he opened his mouth again, five hundred thousand.

And my arm had never looked more beautiful.

The house didn't take long to sell. I used one of those companies that box everything up for you, I wouldn't need much of my own, nowhere to put it even if I did. I made the children take their old toys and school books from the attic, the things they assumed I'd keep forever, the free storage of a mother's heart.

Two months later I went back to the shop. I asked the young man about the bracelet that had been in the window, he remembered me, said had I come to try it on again. He was humouring me, prepared to be kind, because why not?

I said no, I didn't need to try it on. I would take it, there and then, no need to wrap.

I had the phone numbers with me, bank account details, it was a simple matter of transferring funds.

My arm has never looked more beautiful.

I live at the end of your street. I am not an old lady, but I do have five grown children, and I wear their inheritance on my arm. When the weather is bad, I go to them, the children who now have to keep rooms for me. I'm a good guest, I always make my bed, never raid the fridge, and haven't once come home at three am, drunk, sobbing that he or she doesn't love me, before throwing up in the hall. Not yet.

They'd like me to get it insured, but I ask what's the point? It's always with me, and I am always where I am. Here, now.

The house was lovely, but I was not married to the house. I was married to him. and he is dead. I am his widow. And I was never a very good house-wife.

Now – look at my wrist, see the delicious depth of thirteen emeralds, diamonds linked between, couldn't you just dive in? Couldn't you? Wouldn't you?

You'll never look more beautiful.

I did.

JAIL BAIT

Jɪʟʟ's ᴛᴇʟʟɪɴɢ ᴍᴇ the girl unit at Holloway is the coolest thing she's ever heard of. Special and new made and all shiny and clean. And just for us. It was on the radio – I didn't hear it, I don't listen to that kind of radio, don't listen to any kind of radio, got enough voices of my own to listen to, tell the truth – but Jill heard about it and she told me and we thought it was just so fucking cool. It's not got any of the old bitches in it, sad old slags and the slappers who've been around forever anyway and don't know where else to be, except just this side of North London, downwind of Hampstead, turn back if you get to Arsenal, you've gone too far. You've always got to go too far.

Getting our first tattoos together. Real tattoos, paid for and sterile and everything. Watching the man painting on her skin, soft flesh raised into hoarse red welts, wiping away the blood and adding new colour, pretty yellow and blue and deep red darker than her blood. Then my turn and Jill said it wouldn't hurt, didn't hurt her, did it? She wasn't whimpering for fuck's sake. So I took off my bra, lay down, heart shape over heart space. But it did hurt. Too fucking much. I made him stop even though she said I couldn't. Made him give up halfway through. He said I must have a low pain threshold. Maybe I do. I also have a tattoo of a broken heart.

Sitting in Jill's bedroom – also kitchen, lounge, bathroom,

the lot – sitting on the floor, leaning against her knees, hoping if I wait here long enough she might stroke my head again, play with my hair. She doesn't. We're sitting there and then she says how fucking crap the end of daylight saving is, how she can't stand it and now the bloody sun's coming in waking her at eight in the morning and then it's dark by four, dark before the day's even started and too damn cold and what the fuck are we supposed to do for Christmas dinner anyway? I thought it was a big leap from the end of October to the full stuffed turkey, flaming Christmas pudding, but you could see what she meant. Then she said we should go to Holloway. For the festive season. And I'm like fuck me but you're a mad cunt, madder than I am, and Jill says that's just not possible, just not possible. But she's not making a whole lot of sense either, she can't mean it, that place fucking stinks and anyway last time we tried that shit she got to Holloway, I ended up in bloody Styal, two weeks out of my mind in boredom valley and then luckily just about loopy enough to get shunted off to community care hole. Left there in a halfway house to nowhere, easily influenced, just keep the mad fucker on the medication and she'll be good as gold, good as Goldilocks, steal your fucking porridge you stupid great cunts and what do you mean I can't see her, I have to see her, who else is there? Then fuck you bitch and now what's the problem, you've got another eye haven't you? Oh Christ and such a lot of fucking blood and God I hope it's not mine, there's nothing like an institutionalised period to start the day, end the day, start the week – more radio fucking shite – and then the quiet and the sweet icecream and jellies, temazepam baby I am, will be, ever be, hush now good girl.

Anyway, anyway, the point being that the last time we tried

to come in from the cold they tore us apart and broke my heart and Jill came tumbling after. But apparently ... Holloway's got this new young offenders unit and the radio lady from the north think's that's shit, thinks all the money will go there, showcase for the dangerous young ones, too much of a good thing and what about the poor little girls in the frozen north, where will all their good money go? Stay down here baby, warm in the soft south where it always has been, did you not notice it's why we moved here too? So – it's the end of October. We just have to do it well enough, big but not too big, within the next couple of weeks, then the least it'll be is remand and maybe even a few months more to get us all the way into spring, fever of the recently freed.

But we have to do it right. Too big and we'll not see summer soon enough. Too small and it's crap cell night, maybe a caution, and worse than that the possibility of another fucking year fucking the carers. So whoring's out because that's always leading back to some foster daddy, let me hold you and make it all better baby, oh yes please do, that's just what I need. And shoplifting's good for the clothes, or the dinner, or even just the sheer fucking thrill of being bad in the shining light of security cameras and in the face of Henry Stupid the thick cunt who stands at the door pretending to be a security guard, biceps for brains and a dick the size of my clit, but shoplifting won't get us Christmas crackers with plastic scissors inside. And housebreaking is possible but Jill's still terrified of dogs and gets tinnitus with too much loud noise – or a too hard smack on the head – and if we want them to get us it would have to be dog or alarm and what's the point of the pointless break-in if you get away with it? Indeed.

First break-in. We were thirteen, fourteen at the most. Maybe Jill was already fourteen. Fast shared a gram of speed and running around the town, new town with walkways turned into airplane runaways, ready to fucking take off there was so much of the too-much energy spilling round my veins. Then Jill says we should use the excess and do a job. She's been watching daytime re-runs of The Sweeney, *it takes me a minute to work out what she's talking about. There's a place on the corner, a flat above the closed off-licence, the woman who lives there works every day, gets the bus first thing and isn't back until dark. She'll be safely at the office. It's easy to get in. No dog, no alarm, she's probably not even thirty yet that woman, no money for any good security shit. Good guess, no security at all, but she's got a great place. Easy in through the back window and it's nice in there. Just bedroom and lounge, kitchen and bathroom. And all of it girlie soft and warm, too much pink, but it'll do us. We eat bacon and eggs – Jill can't eat much, but speed's never really affected my appetite, I'm weird like that. I can just soak those drugs right up. She does me a big breakfast – half a packet of bacon, three eggs just how I like them, yolk running all over the bacon, bright yellow into the setting fat, geography rivulets on the plate. Bacon's a bit too salty, smoked back, but good anyway. I chew the rind and walk through the little flat. We think about a place like this, maybe Jill and I could get a place together, share it. The woman's got chocolates in her fridge, creme eggs too, we take the telly into the bedroom and get into bed, sheets quite clean, must have been changed only a few days ago and no fucking or period stains, maybe she's got a washing machine, easier that way to wash your sheets whenever you want to. We eat choco-*

late and watch Richard and Judy, laugh at the phone-in moan-
in, but then it's too comfortable and warm and we fall asleep
and we've got problems of our own. It's dark, the only light is
from the telly, the woman's walked in and guess who's sleeping
in her bed and she's off on one and screaming at us, hitting at
us and I don't know what the fuck she's so pissed off for, we
didn't take anything. Jill can't believe she's hitting her and I
can't believe she's hitting Jill, can't she see how stupid that is?
She's fucking lucky we fell asleep, we were going to take loads
of shit and we didn't so what's the fucking problem? What is
your fucking problem you stupid fucking ignorant bitch? Big
dry cleaning bill I expect. Hard work getting all that blood off
the pretty pink duvet in your basic home washing machine.
The woman moved out weekend after that. Squatters moved
in. Bet they didn't keep it as nice as she did.

Jill rolls a joint, mostly tobacco, thin rub of hash into it,
then special treat for the goodest of good girls, sprinkling of
coke across the top – she worked last night in the City boy
street, sweet rich boys paying in kind. Kind City boy forced
to hand over cash too when Jill explained what was going
to happen when she stopped twisting his balls and the blood
flooded back in and then out again when she used the blade
hidden in her other hand. Fifty quid, just like that. Scared City
boy pissing in his own wind. But driving home anyway. Whimpering back to his girlfriend and just an especially difficult day
in the money markets darling, I'm a bit tired, maybe I'll have
a little lie down. No you bitch, don't fucking touch me there,
I didn't mean that kind of a lie down, for fuck's sake, is that
all you bloody women ever think about? Jill and I lie back and
dream of Holloway, special shared room and painted walls and

breakfast and lunch and dinner and hide out in the house of girlies until summer comes around. I'm wondering, just briefly, if Jill's got this completely right, if it's all going to be so fucking lovely, I mean the point is, it is a house of detention right? But she's sure it must be great because otherwise why would the Tory bitch on the radio be so fucking concerned and anyway, even if it's just like the same old place, no new paint job or anything, if it isn't for the old ones, if it's just for us, then think of how it will be, no old lady smells and no mad mothers crying for their fostered babies and the following, always following because we're always the little ones. We'll be big girls, just us, our very own home from home. Which, when the home you're homing from is ten foot square of peeling damp and the screams of the dozy cunt next door who will keep welcoming him into her bed and then getting surprised when she finds his fist into her face as well, if that's home and Jack Frost is on his way, then maybe anything's better. Or maybe I just wanted Jill to stroke my hair again. Like she did. Just the once. Soft stroking like she meant it, not absent action like I might have been the cat or her own head in need of a good itch. Anyway, anyway, the hash is spreading my mind all over the fucking place, it's chocolate spread brain, and then because neither of us smokes tobacco if we can help it, we're getting a nicotine rush too and I'm just starting to refocus when the pretty little truth drug kicks in on top of all that and my poor bitch of a brain doesn't know what to do. Mouth opens and closes and doesn't know if it should laugh or talk and starts to say words, any will do, but tobacco dries my lips and nothing comes out just a goo gah of bollocks and pretty soon Jill thinks I'm really funny, really fucking funny and I so want her not to laugh at me, I want that hand to stroke my head not point fucking laughing at me.

First time laughing, too stoned, new to us, first time laughing so much, giggling stoned laughter and it won't go away and I've peed my pants and Jill and me both just laughing even more at that, sticky ammonia turning cold in my jeans. She's trying to cut out a line of speed to sharpen me up, take the edge off the giggle, but her hand's shaking so much and I'm laughing so much I blow it all over the table. Stopped me laughing though.

Nothing to stop her laughing at me now and I'm not wasting good drugs on her sense of humour this time. So I'm fucked off and hate her. Hate her hard. Worried by the hate, it's the one that scares me, and I really don't like to hate Jill, but she is so not going to stop laughing, she's having far too good a fucking time and I think maybe I need to leave now, go out for a walk, get away from the laughing bitch because I might just have to smack her fucking big mouth if she doesn't stop, and I've never hit Jill before, though she's hit me loads of times and I don't know if I could hit her, not really, but right now I might just slam my fist so far into that laughing gob of hers it'll come out her cunt next time she sees it. I don't like being this angry. Worries me. Don't like it at all. And then – bliss, sweet rapture, and praise the gifts of the virgin who'd hate to see me harm a hair on the beloved's head, I've slammed pissed off hands hard into my pocket and there's a couple of jellies in there with the condoms and the Polo mints. I know, but it only sounds like an odd combination at first. You figure. And then maybe I can just about do this. The jellies and the coke and the hash? I don't know if it's a great combination, it's not quite the real thing, but fuck it I might as well anyway because daylight saving has all gone and it's dark at four thirty now and so we're not going anywhere, right? Wrong.

Jill stops laughing and pulls me out of the door with her. I don't need a coat she says, even though it's bloody freezing, shit sleety rain far too early in November and slashing at my face, but she tells me not to worry, there's a nice warm BMW parked just around the corner and we can put the heater on full and move in for half an hour or so. Jill can't drive but she knows everything else there is to know about cars. How to get through the electric locking system. How to turn off the alarm without a key. How to start the motor. Jill fucked a mechanic for a few months last year, stole his knowledge and fucked off with his new set of tools too. Left his dick, not the best of his tools. And it's a nice car, big and easy to drive. At least it is until Jill starts trying to direct me, over there, that right turn, no not this, the next one, shit you've missed it, u-turn, here, yes of course you can, you fucking well can, don't talk shit, you fucking well can. Fucking well can't. Coke, hash and jellies, power steering power steered from the passenger seat. Straight into an oncoming Nissan. We barely move, the BMW takes the swipe with a fat and solid crunch – side impact bars, air bags as standard, there's something about these company cars that makes even facing the wrong way in rush hour not seem so bad. The tinny little Japanese spins out and then back into the line of traffic, driver looks as if he thinks it might be all right. He's facing the right way. His neck isn't broken. Chassis is though. I'm dazed and Jill's pulling at my hand, grabs me out of my seat and we're running fast, down a couple of dark streets, through a pathway, old lady shrinking against the

wall, holding her trolley to her like a shield, thanking God
we weren't interested. A couple of people chase at first, but
they don't really care. Much more concerned about the guy in
the Nissan than the couple of girls who've pinched some rich
git's car. God knows he'll have enough insurance. I bet Nissan
Man's only third party, he looks like a local. Want to tell Jill,
but she'll hate me for worrying, looking back. Jill doesn't look
back. Quick turn left, no idea of exactly where we're headed
but we know there's a canal along here somewhere, no-one
comes to a canal at dusk. Not unless they're running too. Into
an overgrown estate and thanking winter now, glad of early
sunset. I'm fretting about fingerprints but Jill is so sure that's
irrelevant, bloke'll get his car back and don't the cops have
better to think about than that and who the fuck knows where
we live anyway? No-one. No-one but Jill. We find the canal
and follow the line down towards town, brighter lights and I
really am freezing now, coke rush long gone, just a headache
from too many drugs and the adrenaline mix, temples throbbing, I'm thinking maybe we're headed home, maybe we can
leave it for tonight, back to Jill's and a bag of chips, vinegar
and grease on my hands until the morning, but Jill sees me
shivering and my goose-pimpled skin takes her ahead to the
turkey. She wants us safe and warm for Christmas. Tucked up
cosy and waiting for Santa. Inside.

*First Christmas alone. The mother and father have gone
away. Packed their car with a DNA-variegation of children
and driven to their cousins in the north. And I will not go
with them. I will not go to the happy family and play the good
child. We have been fighting for weeks and then she said it, the
mother, OK, don't come, we'll take the others. You stay here.*

By yourself. That's fine. She turned the electricity off as she left and removed the key card. Christmas morning listening to the one radio in the house that had batteries and boiling milk for hot weetabix, grateful for the gas stove. I'm eleven, Jill's twelve and a half. She knocks on the door, shivering in pyjamas and dressing gown. Her lot are still asleep and can she watch telly at my place, she knows we have too many kids here for them to attempt the sort of TV rules they have at her house. No TV. Jill can't believe it, is shocked – all alone? Stunned – they've really left you all alone? And so fucking excited. Stays all morning. By eleven we've finished the Baileys and started on the Tia Maria. Weetabix with hot milk and whisky. Her gran swears by whisky to keep you well, milk to line the stomach, makes Jill a hot toddy every night in winter. Jill says it will stop us getting sick. It doesn't, but we're not bothered. Morecombe and Wise are probably on telly now, it doesn't matter. Queen's Message comes and goes and Jill still isn't going home, she's having too much fun and I do think, I really do, that maybe her gran will be worried, but then the thought passes and anyway, she won't know to find Jill here, thinks my lot are all away. They are. Early evening and there's Advocaat and some cheery cherry brandy and Jill thinks we should set fire to a pudding. But we haven't got a Christmas pudding, so it's the last of the Weetabix and a third of a bottle goes on top, because there's alcohol in Christmas pudding too, isn't there? So it can't matter how much we throw on. Can't matter until the lit Weetabix flies up to the greasy nets and we've left the gas on to heat the place and there's a lot of flame, lot of fire and we run out to the balcony, Jill screaming, nylon dressing gowns glowing in the night wind. Hospital, new homes, new parents, Jill's gran can't cope and she joins me in care limbo.

Until that Christmas Jill had only been my best friend. After that she was my only friend.

We're out now, so we may as well stay out. We may as well make it happen tonight. That's Jill's plan. Along the canal for a bit, past a couple of girls out working. Not looking for work, actually working. Jill gives a few pointers to the one giving a blow job. 'Slower love, slower. The gentle gobble's what the bloke's after, aren't you mate?' Punter and girl look up, Jill's smiling, as much as you can smile with your gob wide open miming the mouthing. The girl slows down, the punter nod relief and grins, winks at Jill. The kid's probably only about fourteen, no fucking idea yet. 'That's it love. You've got him now. He's happy now. well done love, that's it, keep on, good girl.' The bloke's smiling, eyes closed, pants down. Jill reaches for his wallet, poking out of his trouser pocket, grabs a twenty for herself and pushes another into the girl's bra top. Poor bitch must be freezing. All the while Jill's sweet talking the pair of them through it. 'Now you've got it, good girl, that's the way. Soft and slow. See love, there's some things your mum'll never teach you.' He's grinning and moaning to himself and the girl's sucking and slobbering for all she's worth, eyes wide and delighted. We walk on, maybe ten yards and once we're almost at the bridge Jill shouts out, 'That's it! Good girl. You're doing a great job, great job. Soft and slow and get them going and now -' The girl looks up, mouth full, the punter opens his smiling eyes, grateful inquisitive looks towards the pair of us from both of them, 'Now bite the fucker off!' Jill screams with delight, girl chokes with laughter, man freaks, cock shrivels, nothing to blow. God knows why they do it, men are a fuck of a lot braver than us. I'd never trust anything that tender to the teeth of a stranger. We run off and Jill can't get over herself, fucking delighted she is. Twenty quid richer too.

First trick. Jill's idea. We've both done it, Jill figures we might as well start getting paid for it. Jill figures. I'm fifteen, she's sixteen. Legal. Real. I'm nervous about it though so she tells me to watch her, see how she goes and if she can do it, then so can I. A fuck's a fuck, right? And I can just stop with a blow job if I really want to. I don't know. Seems to me your actual fuck – eyes closed, all noise and panting – is a damn sight less personal than having some stranger's dick in my mouth. Anyway, she's street-cornering herself and I'm stopping in the dark part, under the arches, watching her and these lads come up. It's a stag party. They want her for the groom. What'll she do for twenty quid? We didn't know much about market forces at the time. She offered the lot. Quite a show, best man got a handjob, bride's little brother got a blowjob and then Jill's feeling a bit knackered so she calls me out of the corner and asks the groom how does he fancy me and her together? This is all out in the fucking street, mind. Anyway, course he does. So I'm there right and Jill reckons it'll be fine and then we're fooling about and now the groom's got his dick out and Jill reckons I should do him, get it over with, at least she's there with me. So I turn to do him and then I see it's all of them that are waiting. Not just the groom and this wasn't the deal and Jill's saying no, this wasn't the deal, but that's not the fucking point, right? The best man's not quite so drunk now. She did half a dozen of them and I did six of the others. This was not voluntary. Except when they left the little brother ran back and gave us another twenty each. So it wasn't really rape either. Was it? We got better at it after that. More fucking careful anyway.

So I'm thinking about that girl and how I'm so bloody happy to be running round winter with Jill and not on my knees by the canal and we're coming back up to Holloway Road now and Jill says that's auspicious. It's a sign. Yeah, it's a fucking road sign. Not what she means. And there's lights and cars and a few drunks and some young people in groups, pissed and laughing on their way out for the night, and Jill's speeding now, really fucking speeding, God knows what on. Cold and potential and the twenty quid in her pocket I guess. And she's looking all around and thinking who can we do? What can we do? Then she sees it, other side of the road, furniture shop. And in the window, a bloody fairy tale bed. Really fairy tale. A four poster straight out of 'Sleeping Beauty'. All over girlie shit and frills and pretty and embroidered roses, wide curtains with white flounces and I can't believe that Jill even thinks that looks like anything, but she's just completely taken with it, and they've done some special lighting on it too, it's all soft and golden, glowing in the cold street. And the cover turned down and a silk nightie laid out just waiting for the Princess to float in and sleep forever, no night dancing to wear out her shoes, no hidden pea to bruise her delicate skin. Perfect. And Jill's got a rubbish bin and it just goes right through the window, before I can say not to, before I can even ask what the fuck she's doing and the glass only takes two hits and then it shatters, glass mountain collapses with sparkling prisms all around us, glitter snow on the ground and the ringing of alarm bells. And Jill just takes her time, gives me her clothes, one by one, like I'm the fucking palace maid and I fold them up and put them on the ground because what else can I do and then she's naked and she climbs in through the broken window, glass under her feet but that doesn't matter and I help her put on the nightie and she just gets into bed. Climbs into the bed. I plump up the pillows and tuck her in and kiss her goodnight, pull the curtains around her. I'd turn out the lights but they're flashing blue.

First night in the girl place. It's OK. Really it is. Lots better than I've been in before, that's for sure. It's really not bad. The lady on the radio was right. I mean it is Holloway, but it is pretty flash too. Jill doesn't know though. It all took ages working out what had happened, if they were going to do her or section her. I was easy, accomplice, best friend, no nutter me. Not now. Only then they figured same for her – she was bad, not mad this time. True too. She's not mad. Pissed off but. Jill turned twenty while we were on remand, they reckoned she's too old for this. Too late for it to do her any good. Fucked her off no end. I didn't think it would be all right being here without her. But it's not that bad. Not as bad as I thought anyway.

Still, it'll be summer soon.

TO BRIXTON BEACH

THERE ARE IMAGES in the water. The pool holds them, has held them, since it was built in the thirties and before. And before that too, when there were ponds here, in the park, ponds the locals used to bathe in. Men at first, then men and women, separate bathing times, of course. A pond before the pool, a house with gardens before the park, perhaps a common before that, a field, a forest. We can go back forever. And on, and on.

6am. The first swimmers arrive, absurd to the gym-goers, the yoga-bunnies, those impatient, imperfect bodies readying for the cold, clear, cool.

When Charlie was a boy he and his brother Sid used to run all the way up from Kennington to swim, skipping out in the middle of the night, long hot summer nights, too sweaty in their little room, no mother there to watch over them anyway, sneaking off on their mate Bill's bike, to where the air was fresher, the trees greener, the sky and stars deeper, wider. And the pond so clean, green. Charlie hadn't been to the sea or to the mountains then, but the air in Brockwell Park felt cool enough.

8am, the pre-office rush, pushing at the entrance desk, swimmers to the right, gym-ers to the left, one half to fast breath, hot body, pumping music, the other to cold, cool, clear.

Mid-morning and the local kids begin to arrive. Jayneen

lives in the Barrier Block, in summer she and her friend Elise and Elise's cousin Monique go to the lido every day. They walk along streets named for poets, poets Monique has read too, poets she knows, smart girl, smart mouth an' all, they walk in tiny shorts and tinier tops and they know what they do, and they laugh as they do it, as those boys slow down on the foolish too-small bikes they ride, slow down and look them up, look them lower, look them over. They three are all young woman skin and flesh showing and body ripe. And they know it, love it. The girls walk along and make their way to the lido that is Brixton Beach and they don't bother getting changed, they are not here to swim, Elise spent five hours last weekend getting her hair made fine in rows, tight and fine, she doesn't want to risk chlorine on that, they come to the lido to sit and soak up the sun and the admiring glances. Jayneen looks around, smoothing soft cocoa butter on her skin, as she does twice a day, every day, as she knows to do, and sucks her teeth at the skinny white girl over there by the café, all freckles and burned red, burned dry, silly sitting in the sun. Jayneen's skin is smooth and soft, she's taught Monique too, white girls need to oil their skin too. Maybe white girls need black mothers to teach them how to take care of themselves.

Charlie is in the water. He is already always in the water. Strong powerful strokes pulling him through. He slips past the young men who are running and cartwheeling into the pool, trying to get the girls' attention, trying not to get the life guard's attention, paying no attention to the long low deco lines. The young men look only at the curving lines on young women's bodies. Charlie finds himself thinking of young women and turns his attention back to water, to swimming hard and remembering how to breathe in water. He swims fast and strong up to the shallow end, avoids the squealing, screeching little ones, babes in arms, and turns back, to power on down, alone.

Lunchtime, the place is full. Midday office escapees, retired schoolteachers and half of Brixton market, rolled up Railton Road to get to the green, the water, the blue. One end of the café's outdoor tables over-taken with towels and baby bottles and children's soft toys, floating girls and boys in the water with the yummy mummies, wet mummies, hold me mummy, hold me.

Two babies hanging on to each arm. Helen can't believe it. This is not what she'd planned when she booked that first maternity leave, four years ago. Can it really be so long? She looks at her left hand where Sophia and her play-date Cassandra jump up and down, pumping her arm for dear life, (dear god, who calls their daughter Cassandra? Foretelling the doom of the south London middle classes), while in her right arm she rocks the little rubber ring that Gideon and Katsuki hang on to. Helen shakes her head. Back in the day. Back in the office, loving those days in the office, she wondered what it would feel like, to be one of them, the East Dulwich mummies clogging cafés and footpaths with their designer buggies. She looks up as a shadow crosses her, it is Imogen, Cassandra's mother. Imogen is pointing to the table, surrounded by buggies. Their friends wave, lunch has arrived, Helen passes the children out one by one and immediately they start whining, wanting this, wanting that, she can feel the looks, the disapproval from the swimmers who have come here for quiet and peace. Helen has become that mother. The one with the designer buggy. And she hates the lookers for making her feel it, and hates that she feels it. And she wouldn't give her up babies for anything. And they do need a buggy, and a big one at that, they're twins. (At least she didn't call them Castor and Pollux.) Helen can't win and she knows it. Sits down to her veggie burger. Orders a glass of wine anyway. After all.

Charlie swims, back and forth, back and forth. He lurches into the next lane to avoid the young men dive-bombing to impress the girls and irritate the life guards, makes his perfect turns between two young women squealing at the cold water. He swerves around slower swimmers, through groups of chattering children, he does not stop. Charlie is held in the water, only in the water.

3pm, a mid-afternoon lull. Margaret and Esther sit against the far wall, in direct sunlight, they have been here for five hours, moving to follow the sun. From inside the yoga studio they can hear the slow in and out breaths, the sounds of bodies pulled and pushed into perfection. At seventy-six and eighty-one Margaret and Esther do not worry about perfection, though Margaret still has good legs and Esther is proud of her full head of perfectly white hair. Margaret looks down at her body, the sagging and whole right breast, the missing left. She had the mastectomy fifteen years ago, they spoke to her about reconstruction, but she wasn't much interested, nor in the prosthesis. Margaret likes her body as it is, scars, grey hair, wrinkles, lived. She and Esther have been coming to the pool every summer, three times a week for fifty years, bar that bad patch when the council closed it in the 80s. They swim twenty lengths together, heads above the water, a slow breaststroke side by side because Esther likes to chat and keep her lovely hair dry. Then Esther gets out and Margaret swims another twenty herself, head down this time, breathing out in the water, screaming out in the water sometimes, back then, when it was harder, screaming in the water because it was the only time Esther couldn't hear her cry. It's better now, she is alive and delighted to be here, glad to be sharing another summer with the love of her life. Esther passes her a slice of ginger cake, buttered, and they sit back to watch the water. Two old ladies, holding age-spotted hands.

Charlie swims on.

5.30pm, just before the after-office rush. In the changing rooms, Ameena takes a deep breath as she unwraps her swimming costume from her towel. She sent away for it a week ago, when she knew she could no longer deny herself the water. It arrived yesterday. It is a beautiful, deep blue. It makes her think of water even to touch it, the texture is soft, silky. She has been hot for days, wants to give herself over to the water, to the pool. She slowly takes off her own clothes and replaces them as she does with the deep blue costume. When she has dressed in the two main pieces – swim pants and tunic – she goes to the mirror to pull on the hood, fully covering her hair. Three little girls stand and stare unashamedly. She smiles at them and takes the bravery of their stare for herself, holds her covered head high, walks through the now-quiet changing room, eyes glancing her way, conversations lowered, walks out to the pool in her deep blue burkini. Ameena loved swimming at school, has been denying herself the water since she decided to dress in full hijab. She does not want to deny herself any more. The burkini is her choice, the water her desire. She can have both, and will brave the stares to do so. In the water, Ameena looks like any other woman in a wetsuit, swims better than most, and gives herself over to the repetitive mantra that are her arms and legs, heart and lungs, working in unison. It is almost prayer and she is grateful.

Charlie swims two, three, four lengths in time with Ameena, and then their rhythm changes, one is out of sync with the other, they are separate again.

8pm, the café is almost full, the pool almost empty, a last few swimmers, defying the imploring calls of the lifeguards. Time to close up, time to get out. Diners clink wine glasses and look through fairy lights past the lightly-stirring water to the gym, people on treadmills, on step machines, in ballet and spin classes. Martin and Ayo order another beer each and shake their heads. They chose food and beer tonight. And will probably do so again tomorrow evening, they are well matched, well met.

It is quiet and dark night. Charlie swims on, unnoticed. Eventually the café is closed, the gym lights turned off, the cleaners have been and gone, the pool and the park are silent but for the foxes telling the night, tolling the hours with their screams. And a cat, watching.

Charlie climbs from the water now, his body his own again, reassembled from the wishing and the tears and the could be, might be, would be, from hope breathed out into water, from the grins of young men and the laughter of old women and the helpless, rolling giggles of toddlers on soft towels. Remade through summer laughter spilling over the poolside. He dresses. White shirt, long pants, baggy trousers falling over his toes, a waistcoat, tie just-spotted, just-knotted below the turned-up collar, then the too-tight jacket, his big shoes. Without the cane and the moustache and the bowler hat he was just another man, moving at his own pace, quietly through the water. With them, he is himself again. The Little Tramp walking away, back to Kennington, retracing the path he and Sid ran through summer nights to the welcome ponds of Brockwell Park.

Behind him the water holds the memory of a man moving through it in cool midnight, a celluloid pool in which he flickers to life, and is gone.

ACKNOWLEDGEMENTS

Thank you to Carine Osment, Jen Hamilton-Emery, and to Twitter for making the links.

Writing short stories is a fine thing for many reasons – one of those reasons is simply that they are much shorter than novels. Commissioning stories however, and compiling anthologies is a far harder task. I know this having done it myself. There are contracts and payments, chasing up recalcitrant writers and persuading publishers that yes, they do want another anthology and that yes, there will be readers. So to all those who have ever asked me to write a short story, thank you. And to the readers of the short story – thank you. The short story is regularly described as enjoying a revival, for some of us, it never went away. You readers – we readers – are the reason we know it is here to stay.

The stories in this collection first appeared as follows:
    'Martha Grace', published in *Tart Noir*, Pan Macmillan, 2002.
    'From the River's Mouth', broadcast on BBC Radio 4, 2008.
    'Everything is Moving, Everything is Joined', published in *Litmus*, Comma Press, 2011.

Acknowledgements

'No', published in *Blue Lightening*, Slow Dancer Press, 1998.

'Ladies' Fingers', from *The Hand*, Gay Sweatshop, performed 1996.

'*Un bon repas doit commencer par la faim . . .*' published in *Paris Noir*, *Capital Crime Fiction*, Serpent's Tail 2008.

'A Swimmer's Tale', published in *Girls Night In*, Harper Collins, 2000.

'Being the Baroness', published in *Little Black Dress*, Polygon, 2005.

'A Partridge in a Pear Tree', published in *12 Days*, Virago, 2004.

'Siren Songs', first published in *Girls Night In*, Harlequin, 2004.

'The Gilder's Apprentice', published in *The Independent*, 2012.

'Uncertainties and Small Surprises', published in *Fresh Blood*, Do Not Press, 1996.

'Stick Figures', published in *Pretext*, 2001.

'Silk Lovers', published in *Velocity*, Black Spring Press, 2004.

'Face Value', published in *OxCrimes*, Profile, 2014.

'Come Away With Me', published in *The Mammoth Book of Best British Crime 10*, 2013.

'There Is An Old Lady Who Lives Down Our Street', broadcast on *The Verb*, BBC Radio 3, 2011.

'Jail Bait', published in *Britpulp*, Sceptre, 1999.

'To Brixton Beach', broadcast on BBC Radio 4, 2011.